A Thief in the Night

by

E. W. Hornung

The Echo Library 2007

Published by

The Echo Library

Echo Library
131 High St.
Teddington
Middlesex TW11 8HH

www.echo-library.com

Please report serious faults in the text to complaints@echo-library.com

ISBN 1-40681-553-5

Out of Paradise

If I must tell more tales of Raffles, I can but back to our earliest days together, and fill in the blanks left by discretion in existing annals. In so doing I may indeed fill some small part of an infinitely greater blank, across which you may conceive me to have stretched my canvas for the first frank portrait of my friend. The whole truth cannot harm him now. I shall paint in every wart. Raffles was a villain, when all is written; it is no service to his memory to glaze the fact; yet I have done so myself before to-day. I have omitted whole heinous episodes. I have dwelt unduly on the redeeming side. And this I may do again, blinded even as I write by the gallant glamour that made my villain more to me than any hero. But at least there shall be no more reservations, and as an earnest I shall make no further secret of the greatest wrong that even Raffles ever did me.

I pick my words with care and pain, loyal as I still would be to my friend, and yet remembering as I must those Ides of March when he led me blindfold into temptation and crime. That was an ugly office, if you will. It was a moral bagatelle to the treacherous trick he was to play me a few weeks later. The second offence, on the other hand, was to prove the less serious of the two against society, and might in itself have been published to the world years ago. There have been private reasons for my reticence. The affair was not only too intimately mine, and too discreditable to Raffles. One other was involved in it, one dearer to me than Raffles himself, one whose name shall not even now be sullied by association with ours.

Suffice it that I had been engaged to her before that mad March deed. True, her people called it "an understanding," and frowned even upon that, as well they might. But their authority was not direct; we bowed to it as an act of politic grace; between us, all was well but my unworthiness. That may be gauged when I confess that this was how the matter stood on the night I gave a worthless check for my losses at baccarat, and afterward turned to Raffles in my need. Even after that I saw her sometimes. But I let her guess that there was more upon my soul than she must ever share, and at last I had written to end it all. I remember that week so well! It was the close of such a May as we had never had since, and I was too miserable even to follow the heavy scoring in the papers. Raffles was the only man who could get a wicket up at Lord's, and I never once went to see him play. Against Yorkshire, however, he helped himself to a hundred runs as well; and that brought Raffles round to me, on his way home to the Albany.

"We must dine and celebrate the rare event," said he. "A century takes it out of one at my time of life; and you, Bunny, you look quite as much in need of your end of a worthy bottle. Suppose we make it the Caf, Royal, and eight sharp? I'll be there first to fix up the table and the wine."

And at the Caf, Royal I incontinently told him of the trouble I was in. It was the first he had ever heard of my affair, and I told him all, though not before our bottle had been succeeded by a pint of the same exemplary brand. Raffles heard me out with grave attention. His sympathy was the more grateful for the tactful brevity with which it was indicated rather than expressed. He only wished that I had told him of this complication in the beginning; as I had not, he agreed with me that the only course was a candid and complete renunciation. It was not as though my divinity had a penny of her own, or I could earn an honest one. I had explained to Raffles that she was an orphan, who spent most of her time with an aristocratic aunt in the country, and the remainder under the repressive roof of a pompous politician in Palace Gardens. The aunt had, I believed, still a sneaking softness for me, but her illustrious brother had set his face against me from the first.

"Hector Carruthers!" murmured Raffles, repeating the detested name with his clear, cold eye on mine. "I suppose you haven't seen much of him?"

"Not a thing for ages," I replied. "I was at the house two or three days last year, but they've neither asked me since nor been at home to me when I've called. The old beast seems a judge of men."

And I laughed bitterly in my glass.

"Nice house?" said Raffles, glancing at himself in his silver cigarette-case.

"Top shelf," said I. "You know the houses in Palace Gardens, don't you?"

"Not so well as I should like to know them, Bunny."

"Well, it's about the most palatial of the lot. The old ruffian is as rich as Croesus. It's a country-place in town."

"What about the window-fastenings?" asked Raffles casually.

I recoiled from the open cigarette-case that he proffered as he spoke. Our eyes met; and in his there was that starry twinkle of mirth and mischief, that sunny beam of audacious devilment, which had been my undoing two months before, which was to undo me as often as he chose until the chapter's end. Yet for once I withstood its glamour; for once I turned aside that luminous glance with front of steel. There was no need for Raffles to voice his plans. I read them all between the strong lines of his smiling, eager face. And I pushed back my chair in the equal eagerness of my own resolve.

"Not if I know it!" said I. "A house I've dined in—a house I've seen her in—a house where she stays by the month together! Don't put it into words, Raffles, or I'll get up and go."

"You mustn't do that before the coffee and liqueur," said Raffles laughing. "Have a small Sullivan first: it's the royal road to a cigar. And now let me observe that your scruples would do you honor if old Carruthers still lived in the house in question."

"Do you mean to say he doesn't?"

Raffles struck a match, and handed it first to me. "I mean to say, my dear Bunny, that Palace Gardens knows the very name no more. You began by telling me you had heard nothing of these people all this year. That's quite enough to account for our little misunderstanding. I was thinking of the house, and you were thinking of the people in the house."

"But who are they, Raffles? Who has taken the house, if old Carruthers has moved, and how do you know that it is still worth a visit?"

"In answer to your first question—Lord Lochmaben," replied Raffles, blowing bracelets of smoke toward the ceiling. "You look as though you had never heard of him; but as the cricket and racing are the only part of your paper that you condescend to read, you can't be expected to keep track of all the peers created in your time. Your other question is not worth answering. How do you suppose that I know these things? It's my business to get to know them, and that's all there is to it. As a matter of fact, Lady Lochmaben has just as good diamonds as Mrs. Carruthers ever had; and the chances are that she keeps them where Mrs. Carruthers kept hers, if you could enlighten me on that point."

As it happened, I could, since I knew from his niece that it was one on which Mr. Carruthers had been a faddist in his time. He had made quite a study of the cracksman's craft, in a resolve to circumvent it with his own. I remembered myself how the ground-floor windows were elaborately bolted and shuttered, and how the doors of all the rooms opening upon the square inner hall were fitted with extra Yale locks, at an unlikely height, not to be discovered by one within the room. It had been the butler's business to turn and to collect all these keys before retiring for the night. But the key of the safe in the study was supposed to be in the jealous keeping of the master of the house himself. That safe was in its turn so ingeniously hidden that I never should have found it for myself. I well remember how one who showed it to me (in the innocence of her heart) laughed as she assured me that even her little trinkets were solemnly locked up in it every night. It had been let into the wall behind one end of the book-case, expressly to preserve the barbaric splendor of Mrs. Carruthers; without a doubt these Lochmabens would use it for the same purpose; and in the altered circumstances I had no hesitation in giving Raffles all the information he desired. I even drew him a rough plan of the ground-floor on the back of my menu-card.

"It was rather clever of you to notice the kind of locks on the inner doors," he remarked as he put it in his pocket. "I suppose you don't remember if it was a Yale on the front door as well?"

"It was not," I was able to answer quite promptly. "I happen to know because I once had the key when—when we went to a theatre together."

"Thank you, old chap," said Raffles sympathetically. "That's all I shall want from you, Bunny, my boy. There's no night like to-night!"

It was one of his sayings when bent upon his worst. I looked at him aghast. Our cigars were just in blast, yet already he was signalling for his bill. It was impossible to remonstrate with him until we were both outside in the street.

"I'm coming with you," said I, running my arm through his.

"Nonsense, Bunny!"

"Why is it nonsense? I know every inch of the ground, and since the house has changed hands I have no compunction. Besides, 'I have been there' in the other sense as well: once a thief, you know! In for a penny, in for a pound!"

It was ever my mood when the blood was up. But my old friend failed to appreciate the characteristic as he usually did. We crossed Regent Street in silence. I had to catch his sleeve to keep a hand in his inhospitable arm.

"I really think you had better stay away," said Raffles as we reached the other curb. "I've no use for you this time."

"Yet I thought I had been so useful up to now?"

"That may be, Bunny, but I tell you frankly I don't want you to-night."

"Yet I know the ground and you don't! I tell you what," said I: "I'll come just to show you the ropes, and I won't take a pennyweight of the swag."

Such was the teasing fashion in which he invariably prevailed upon me; it was delightful to note how it caused him to yield in his turn. But Raffles had the grace to give in with a laugh, whereas I too often lost my temper with my point.

"You little rabbit!" he chuckled. "You shall have your share, whether you come or not; but, seriously, don't you think you might remember the girl?"

"What's the use?" I groaned. "You agree there is nothing for it but to give her up. I am glad to say that for myself before I asked you, and wrote to tell her so on Sunday. Now it's Wednesday, and she hasn't answered by line or sign. It's waiting for one word from her that's driving me mad."

"Perhaps you wrote to Palace Gardens?"

"No, I sent it to the country. There's been time for an answer, wherever she may be."

We had reached the Albany, and halted with one accord at the Piccadilly portico, red cigar to red cigar.

"You wouldn't like to go and see if the answer's in your rooms?" he asked.

"No. What's the good? Where's the point in giving her up if I'm going to straighten out when it's too late? It is too late, I have given her up, and I am coming with you!"

The hand that bowled the most puzzling ball in England (once it found its length) descended on my shoulder with surprising promptitude.

"Very well, Bunny! That's finished; but your blood be on your own pate if evil comes of it. Meanwhile we can't do better than turn in here till you have finished your cigar as it deserves, and topped up with such a cup of tea as you must learn to like if you hope to get on in your new profession. And when the hours are small enough, Bunny, my boy, I don't mind admitting I shall be very glad to have you with me."

I have a vivid memory of the interim in his rooms. I think it must have been the first and last of its kind that I was called upon to sustain with so much knowledge of what lay before me. I passed the time with one restless eye upon the clock, and the other on the Tantalus which Raffles ruthlessly declined to unlock. He admitted that it was like waiting with one's pads on; and in my slender experience of the game of which he was a world's master, that was an ordeal not to be endured without a general quaking of the inner man. I was, on the other hand, all right when I got to the metaphorical wicket; and half the surprises that Raffles sprung on me were doubtless due to his early recognition of the fact.

On this occasion I fell swiftly and hopelessly out of love with the prospect I had so gratuitously embraced. It was not only my repugnance to enter that house in that way, which grew upon my better judgment as the artificial enthusiasm of the evening evaporated from my veins. Strong as that repugnance became, I had an even stronger feeling that we were embarking on an important enterprise far too much upon the spur of the moment. The latter qualm I had the temerity to confess to Raffles; nor have I often loved him more than when he freely admitted it to be the most natural feeling in the world. He assured me, however, that he had had my Lady Lochmaben and her jewels in his mind for several months; he had sat behind them at first nights; and long ago determined what to take or to reject; in fine, he had only been waiting for those topographical details which it had been my chance privilege to supply. I now learned that he had numerous houses in a similar state upon his list; something or other was wanting in each case in order to complete his plans. In that of the Bond Street jeweller it was a trusty accomplice; in the present instance, a more intimate knowledge of the house. And lastly, this was a Wednesday night, when the tired legislator gets early to his bed.

How I wish I could make the whole world see and hear him, and smell the smoke of his beloved Sullivan, as he took me into these, the secrets of his infamous trade! Neither look nor language would betray the infamy. As a mere talker, I shall never listen to the like of Raffles on this side of the sod; and his talk was seldom garnished by an oath, never in my remembrance by the unclean word. Then he looked like a man who had dressed to dine out, not like one who had long since dined; for his curly hair, though longer that another's, was never untidy in its length; and these were the days when it was still as black as ink. Nor were there many lines as yet upon the smooth and mobile face; and its frame was still that dear den of disorder and good taste, with the carved book-case, the dresser and chests of still older oak, and the Wattses and Rossettis hung anyhow on the walls.

It must have been one o'clock before we drove in a hansom as far as Kensington Church, instead of getting down at the gates of our private road to ruin. Constitutionally shy of the direct approach, Raffles was further deterred by a ball in full swing at the Empress Rooms, whence potential witnesses were pouring between dances into the cool deserted street. Instead he led me a little way up Church Street, and so through the narrow passage into Palace Gardens. He knew the house as well as I did. We made our first survey from the other side of the road. And the house was not quite in darkness; there was a dim light over the door, a brighter one in the stables, which stood still farther back from the road.

"That's a bit of a bore," said Raffles. "The ladies have been out somewhere—trust them to spoil the show! They would get to bed before the stable folk, but insomnia is the curse of their sex and our profession. Somebody's not home yet; that will be the son of the house; but he's a beauty, who may not come home at all."

"Another Alick Carruthers," I murmured, recalling the one I liked least of all the household, as I remembered it.

"They might be brothers," rejoined Raffles, who knew all the loose fish about town. "Well, I'm not sure that I shall want you after all, Bunny."

"Why not?"

"If the front door's only on the latch, and you're right about the lock, I shall walk in as though I were the son of the house myself."

And he jingled the skeleton bunch that he carried on a chain as honest men carry their latchkeys.

"You forget the inner doors and the safe."

"True. You might be useful to me there. But I still don't like leading you in where it isn't absolutely necessary, Bunny."

"Then let me lead you, I answered, and forthwith marched across the broad, secluded road, with the great houses standing back on either side in their ample gardens, as though the one opposite belonged to me. I thought Raffles had stayed behind, for I never heard him at my heels, yet there he was when I turned round at the gate.

"I must teach you the step," he whispered, shaking his head. "You shouldn't use your heel at all. Here's a grass border for you: walk it as you would the plank! Gravel makes a noise, and flower-beds tell a tale. Wait—I must carry you across this."

It was the sweep of the drive, and in the dim light from above the door, the soft gravel, ploughed into ridges by the night's wheels, threatened an alarm at every step. Yet Raffles, with me in his arms, crossed the zone of peril softly as the pard.

"Shoes in your pocket—that's the beauty of pumps!" he whispered on the step; his light bunch tinkled faintly; a couple of keys he stooped and tried, with the touch of a humane dentist; the third let us into the porch. And as we stood together on the mat, as he was gradually closing the door, a clock within chimed a half-hour in fashion so thrillingly familiar to me that I caught Raffles by the arm. My half-hours of happiness had flown to just such chimes! I looked wildly about me in the dim light. Hat-stand and oak settee belonged equally to my past. And Raffles was smiling in my face as he held the door wide for my escape.

"You told me a lie!" I gasped in whispers.

"I did nothing of the sort," he replied. "The furniture's the furniture of Hector Carruthers; but the house is the house of Lord Lochmaben. Look here!"

He had stooped, and was smoothing out the discarded envelope of a telegram. "Lord Lochmaben," I read in pencil by the dim light; and the case was plain to me on the spot. My friends had let their house, furnished, as anybody but Raffles would have explained to me in the beginning.

"All right," I said. "Shut the door."

And he not only shut it without a sound, but drew a bolt that might have been sheathed in rubber.

In another minute we were at work upon the study-door, I with the tiny lantern and the bottle of rock-oil, he with the brace and the largest bit. The Yale lock he had given up at a glance. It was placed high up in the door, feet above the handle, and the chain of holes with which Raffles had soon surrounded it were bored on a level with his eyes. Yet the clock in the hall chimed again, and two ringing strokes resounded through the silent house before we gained admittance to the room.

Raffle's next care was to muffle the bell on the shuttered window (with a silk handkerchief from the hat-stand) and to prepare an emergency exit by opening first the shutters and then the window itself. Luckily it was a still night, and very little wind came in to embarrass us. He then began operations on the safe, revealed by me behind its folding screen of books, while I stood sentry on the threshold. I may have stood there for a dozen minutes, listening to the loud hall clock and to the gentle dentistry of Raffles in the mouth of the safe behind me, when a third sound thrilled my every nerve. It was the equally cautious opening of a door in the gallery overhead.

I moistened my lips to whisper a word of warning to Raffles. But his ears had been as quick as mine, and something longer. His lantern darkened as I turned my head; next moment I felt his breath upon the back of my neck. It was now too late even for a whisper, and quite out of the question to close the mutilated door. There we could only stand, I on the threshold, Raffles at my elbow, while one carrying a candle crept down the stairs.

The study-door was at right angles to the lowest flight, and just to the right of one alighting in the hall. It was thus impossible for us to see who it was until the person was close abreast of us; but by the rustle of the gown we knew that it was one of the ladies, and dressed just as she had come from theatre or ball. Insensibly I drew back as the candle swam into our field of vision: it had not traversed many inches when a hand was clapped firmly but silently across my mouth.

I could forgive Raffles for that, at any rate! In another breath I should have cried aloud: for the girl with the candle, the girl in her ball-dress, at dead of night, the girl with the letter for the post, was the last girl on God's wide earth whom I should have chosen thus to encounter—a midnight intruder in the very house where I had been reluctantly received on her account!

I forgot Raffles. I forgot the new and unforgivable grudge I had against him now. I forgot his very hand across my mouth, even before he paid me the compliment of removing it. There was the only girl in all the world: I had eyes and brains for no one and for nothing else. She had neither seen nor heard us, had looked neither to the right hand nor the left. But a small oak table stood on the opposite side of the hall; it was to this table that she went. On it was one of those boxes in which one puts one's letters for the post; and she stooped to read by her candle the times at which this box was cleared.

The loud clock ticked and ticked. She was standing at her full height now, her candle on the table, her letter in both hands, and in her downcast face a sweet and pitiful perplexity that drew the tears to my eyes. Through a film I saw her open the envelope so lately sealed and read her letter once more, as though she would have altered it a little at the last. It was too late for that; but of a sudden she plucked a rose from her bosom, and was pressing it in with her letter when I groaned aloud.

How could I help it? The letter was for me: of that I was as sure as though I had been looking over her shoulder. She was as true as tempered steel; there were not two of us to whom she wrote and sent roses at dead of night. It was her one chance of writing to me. None would know that she had written. And she cared enough to soften the reproaches I had richly earned, with a red rose warm from her own warm heart. And there, and there was I, a common thief who had broken in to steal! Yet I was unaware that I had uttered a sound until she looked up, startled, and the hands behind me pinned me where I stood.

I think she must have seen us, even in the dim light of the solitary candle. Yet not a sound escaped her as she peered courageously in our direction; neither did one of us move; but the hall clock went on and on, every tick like the beat of a drum to bring the house about our ears, until a minute must have passed as in some breathless dream. And then came the awakening—with such a knocking and a ringing at the front door as brought all three of us to our senses on the spot.

"The son of the house!" whispered Raffles in my ear, as he dragged me back to the window he had left open for our escape. But as he leaped out first a sharp cry stopped me at the sill. "Get back! Get back! We're trapped!" he cried; and in the single second that I stood there, I saw him fell one officer to the ground, and dart across the lawn with another at his heels. A third came running up to the window. What could I do but double back into the house? And there in the hall I met my lost love face to face.

Till that moment she had not recognized me. I ran to catch her as she all but fell. And my touch repelled her into life, so that she shook me off, and stood gasping: "You, of all men! You, of all men!" until I could bear it no more, but broke again for the study-window. "Not that way—not that way!" she cried in an agony at that. Her hands were upon me now. "In there, in there," she whispered, pointing and pulling me to a mere cupboard under the stairs, where hats and coats were hung; and it was she who shut the door on me with a sob.

Doors were already opening overhead, voices calling, voices answering, the alarm running like wildfire from room to room. Soft feet pattered in the gallery and down the stairs about my very ears. I do not know what made me put on my own shoes as I heard them, but I think that I was ready and even longing to walk out and give myself up. I need not say what and who it was that alone restrained me. I heard her name. I heard them crying to her as though she had fainted. I recognized the detested voice of my bete noir, Alick Carruthers, thick as might be expected of the dissipated dog, yet daring to stutter out her name. And then I heard, without catching, her low reply; it was in answer to the somewhat stern questioning of quite another voice; and from what followed I knew that she had never fainted at all.

"Upstairs, miss, did he? Are you sure?"

I did not hear her answer. I conceive her as simply pointing up the stairs. In any case, about my very ears once more, there now followed such a patter and tramp of bare and booted feet as renewed in me a base fear for my own skin. But voices and feet passed over my head, went up and up, higher and higher;

and I was wondering whether or not to make a dash for it, when one light pair came running down again, and in very despair I marched out to meet my preserver, looking as little as I could like the abject thing I felt.

"Be quick!" she cried in a harsh whisper, and pointed peremptorily to the porch.

But I stood stubbornly before her, my heart hardened by her hardness, and perversely indifferent to all else. And as I stood I saw the letter she had written, in the hand with which she pointed, crushed into a ball.

"Quickly!" She stamped her foot. "Quickly—if you ever cared!"

This in a whisper, without bitterness, without contempt, but with a sudden wild entreaty that breathed upon the dying embers of my poor manhood. I drew myself together for the last time in her sight. I turned, and left her as she wished—for her sake, not for mine. And as I went I heard her tearing her letter into little pieces, and the little pieces falling on the floor.

Then I remembered Raffles, and could have killed him for what he had done. Doubtless by this time he was safe and snug in the Albany: what did my fate matter to him? Never mind; this should be the end between him and me as well; it was the end of everything, this dark night's work! I would go and tell him so. I would jump into a cab and drive there and then to his accursed rooms. But first I must escape from the trap in which he had been so ready to leave me. And on the very steps I drew back in despair. They were searching the shrubberies between the drive and the road; a policeman's lantern kept flashing in and out among the laurels, while a young man in evening-clothes directed him from the gravel sweep. It was this young man whom I must dodge, but at my first step in the gravel he wheeled round, and it was Raffles himself.

"Hulloa!" he cried. "So you've come up to join the dance as well! Had a look inside, have you? You'll be better employed in helping to draw the cover in front here. It's all right, officer—only another gentleman from the Empress Rooms."

And we made a brave show of assisting in the futile search, until the arrival of more police, and a broad hint from an irritable sergeant, gave us an excellent excuse for going off arm-in-arm. But it was Raffles who had thrust his arm through mine. I shook him off as we left the scene of shame behind.

"My dear Bunny!" he exclaimed. "Do you know what brought me back?"

I answered savagely that I neither knew nor cared.

"I had the very devil of a squeak for it," he went on. "I did the hurdles over two or three garden-walls, but so did the flyer who was on my tracks, and he drove me back into the straight and down to High Street like any lamplighter. If he had only had the breath to sing out it would have been all up with me then; as it was I pulled off my coat the moment I was round the corner, and took a ticket for it at the Empress Rooms."

"I suppose you had one for the dance that was going on," I growled. Nor would it have been a coincidence for Raffles to have had a ticket for that or any other entertainment of the London season.

"I never asked what the dance was," he returned. "I merely took the opportunity of revising my toilet, and getting rid of that rather distinctive overcoat, which I shall call for now. They're not too particular at such stages of such proceedings, but I've no doubt I should have seen someone I knew if I had none right in. I might even have had a turn, if only I had been less uneasy about you, Bunny."

"It was like you to come back to help me out," said I. "But to lie to me, and to inveigle me with your lies into that house of all houses—that was not like you, Raffles—and I never shall forgive it or you!"

Raffles took my arm again. We were near the High Street gates of Palace Gardens, and I was too miserable to resist an advance which I meant never to give him an opportunity to repeat.

"Come, come, Bunny, there wasn't much inveigling about it," said he. "I did my level best to leave you behind, but you wouldn't listen to me."

"If you had told me the truth I should have listened fast enough," I retorted. "But what's the use of talking? You can boast of your own adventures after you bolted. You don't care what happened to me."

"I cared so much that I came back to see."

"You might have spared yourself the trouble! The wrong had been done. Raffles—Raffles—don't you know who she was?"

It was my hand that gripped his arm once more.

"I guessed," he answered, gravely enough even for me.

"It was she who saved me, not you," I said. "And that is the bitterest part of all!"

Yet I told him that part with a strange sad pride in her whom I had lost— through him—forever. As I ended we turned into High Street; in the prevailing stillness, the faint strains of the band reached us from the Empress Rooms; and I hailed a crawling hansom as Raffles turned that way.

"Bunny," said he, "it's no use saying I'm sorry. Sorrow adds insult in a case like this—if ever there was or will be such another! Only believe me, Bunny, when I swear to you that I had not the smallest shadow of a suspicion that she was in the house."

And in my heart of hearts I did believe him; but I could not bring myself to say the words.

"You told me yourself that you had written to her in the country," he pursued.

"And that letter!" I rejoined, in a fresh wave of bitterness: "that letter she had written at dead of night, and stolen down to post, it was the one I have been waiting for all these days! I should have got it to-morrow. Now I shall never get it, never hear from her again, nor have another chance in this world or in the next. I don't say it was all your fault. You no more knew that she was there than I did. But you told me a deliberate lie about her people, and that I never shall forgive."

I spoke as vehemently as I could under my breath. The hansom was waiting at the curb.

"I can say no more than I have said," returned Raffles with a shrug. "Lie or no lie, I didn't tell it to bring you with me, but to get you to give me certain information without feeling a beast about it. But, as a matter of fact, it was no lie about old Hector Carruthers and Lord Lochmaben, and anybody but you would have guessed the truth."

"'What is the truth?'"

"I as good as told you, Bunny, again and again."

"Then tell me now."

"If you read your paper there would be no need; but if you want to know, old Carruthers headed the list of the Birthday Honors, and Lord Lochmaben is the title of his choice."

And this miserable quibble was not a lie! My lip curled, I turned my back without a word, and drove home to my Mount Street flat in a new fury of savage scorn. Not a lie, indeed! It was the one that is half a truth, the meanest lie of all, and the very last to which I could have dreamt that Raffles would stoop. So far there had been a degree of honor between us, if only of the kind understood to obtain between thief and thief. Now all that was at an end. Raffles had cheated me. Raffles had completed the ruin of my life. I was done with Raffles, as she who shall not be named was done with me.

And yet, even while I blamed him most bitterly, and utterly abominated his deceitful deed, I could not but admit in my heart that the result was put of all proportion to the intent: he had never dreamt of doing me this injury, or indeed any injury at all. Intrinsically the deceit had been quite venial, the reason for it obviously the reason that Raffles had given me. It was quite true that he had spoken of this Lochmaben peerage as a new creation, and of the heir to it in a fashion only applicable to Alick Carruthers. He had given me hints, which I had been too dense to take, and he had certainly made more than one attempt to deter me from accompanying him on this fatal emprise; had he been more explicit, I might have made it my business to deter him. I could not say in my heart that Raffles had failed to satisfy such honor as I might reasonably expect to subsist between us. Yet it seems to me to require a superhuman sanity always and unerringly to separate cause from effect, achievement from intent. And I, for one, was never quite able to do so in this case.

I could not be accused of neglecting my newspaper during the next few wretched days. I read every word that I could find about the attempted jewel-robbery in Palace Gardens, and the reports afforded me my sole comfort. In the first place, it was only an attempted robbery; nothing had been taken, after all. And then—and then—the one member of the household who had come nearest to a personal encounter with either of us was unable to furnish any description of the man—had even expressed a doubt as to the likelihood of identification in the event of an arrest!

I will not say with what mingled feelings I read and dwelt on that announcement It kept a certain faint glow alive within me until the morning brought me back the only presents I had ever made her. They were books; jewellery had been tabooed by the authorities. And the books came back without a word, though the parcel was directed in her hand.

I had made up my mind not to go near Raffles again, but in my heart I already regretted my resolve. I had forfeited love, I had sacrificed honor, and now I must deliberately alienate myself from the one being whose society might yet be some recompense for all that I had lost. The situation was aggravated by the state of my exchequer. I expected an ultimatum from my banker by every post. Yet this influence was nothing to the other. It was Raffles I loved. It was not the dark life we led together, still less its base rewards; it was the man himself, his gayety, his humor, his dazzling audacity, his incomparable courage and resource. And a very horror of turning to him again in mere need of greed set the seal on my first angry resolution. But the anger was soon gone out of me, and when at length Raffles bridged the gap by coming to me, I rose to greet him almost with a shout.

He came as though nothing had happened; and, indeed, not very many days had passed, though they might have been months to me. Yet I fancied the gaze that watched me through our smoke a trifle less sunny than it had been before. And it was a relief to me when he came with few preliminaries to the inevitable point.

"Did you ever hear from her, Bunny?" he asked.

"In a way," I answered. "We won't talk about it, if you don't mind, Raffles."

"That sort of way!" he exclaimed. He seemed both surprised and disappointed.

"Yes," I said, "that sort of way. It's finished. What did you expect?"

"I don't know," said Raffles. "I only thought that the girl who went so far to get a fellow out of a tight place might go a little farther to keep him from getting into another."

"I don't see why she should," said I, honestly enough, yet with the irritation of a less just feeling deep down in my inmost consciousness.

"Yet you did hear from her?" he persisted.

"She sent me back my poor presents, without a word," I said, "if you call that hearing."

I could not bring myself to own to Raffles that I had given her only books. He asked if I was sure that she had sent them back herself; and that was his last question. My answer was enough for him. And to this day I cannot say whether it was more in relief than in regret that he laid a hand upon my shoulder.

"So you are out of Paradise after all!" said Raffles. "I was not sure, or I should have come round before. Well, Bunny, if they don't want you there, there's a little Inferno in the Albany where you will be as welcome as ever

And still, with all the magic mischief of his smile, there was that touch of sadness which I was yet to read aright.

The Chest of Silver

Like all the tribe of which I held him head, Raffles professed the liveliest disdain for unwieldy plunder of any description; it might be old Sheffield, or it might be solid silver or gold, but if the thing was not to be concealed about the person, he would none whatever of it. Unlike the rest of us, however, in this as in all else, Raffles would not infrequently allow the acquisitive spirit of the mere collector to silence the dictates of professional prudence. The old oak chests, and even the mahogany wine-cooler, for which he had doubtless paid like an honest citizen, were thus immovable with pieces of crested plate, which he had neither the temerity to use nor the hardihood to melt or sell. He could but gloat over them behind locked doors, as I used to tell him, and at last one afternoon I caught him at it. It was in the year after that of my novitiate, a halcyon period at the Albany, when Raffles left no crib uncracked, and I played second-murderer every time. I had called in response to a telegram in which he stated that he was going out of town, and must say good-by to me before he went. And I could only think that he was inspired by the same impulse toward the bronzed salvers and the tarnished teapots with which I found him surrounded, until my eyes lit upon the enormous silver-chest into which he was fitting them one by one.

"Allow me, Bunny! I shall take the liberty of locking both doors behind you and putting the key in my pocket," said Raffles, when he had let me in. "Not that I mean to take you prisoner, my dear fellow; but there are those of us who can turn keys from the outside, though it was never an accomplishment of mine."

"Not Crawshay again?" I cried, standing still in my hat.

Raffles regarded me with that tantalizing smile of his which might mean nothing, yet which often meant so much; and in a flash I was convinced that our most jealous enemy and dangerous rival, the doyen of an older school, had paid him yet another visit.

"That remains to be seen," was the measured reply; "and I for one have not set naked eye on the fellow since I saw him off through that window and left myself for dead on this very spot. In fact, I imagined him comfortably back in jail."

"Not old Crawshay!" said I. "He's far too good a man to be taken twice. I should call him the very prince of professional cracksmen."

"Should you?" said Raffles coldly, with as cold an eye looking into mine. "Then you had better prepare to repel princes when I'm gone."

"But gone where?" I asked, finding a corner for my hat and coat, and helping myself to the comforts of the venerable dresser which was one of our friend's greatest treasures. "Where is it you are off to, and why are you taking this herd of white elephants with you?"

Raffles bestowed the cachet of his smile on my description of his motley plate. He joined me in one of his favorite cigarettes, only shaking a superior head at his own decanter.

"One question at a time, Bunny," said he. "In the first place, I am going to have these rooms freshened up with a potful of paint, the electric light, and the telephone you've been at me about so long."

"Good!" I cried. "Then we shall be able to talk to each other day and night!"

"And get overheard and run in for our pains? I shall wait till you are run in, I think," said Raffles cruelly. "But the rest's a necessity: not that I love new paint or am pining for electric light, but for reasons which I will just breathe in your private ear, Bunny. You must not try to take them too seriously; but the fact is, there is just the least bit of a twitter against me in this rookery of an Albany. It must have been started by that tame old bird, Policeman Mackenzie; it isn't very bad as yet, but it needn't be that to reach my ears. Well, it was open to me either to clear out altogether, and so confirm whatever happened to be in the air, or to go off for a time, under some arrangement which would give the authorities ample excuse for overhauling every inch of my rooms. Which would you have done, Bunny?"

"Cleared out, while I could!" said I devoutly.

"So I should have thought," rejoined Raffles. "Yet you see the merit of my plan. I shall leave every mortal thing unlocked."

"Except that," said I, kicking the huge oak case with the iron bands and clamps, and the baize lining fast disappearing under heavy packages bearing the shapes of urns and candelabra.

"That," replied Raffles, "is neither to go with me nor to remain here."

"Then what do you propose to do with it?"

"You have your banking account, and your banker," he went on. This was perfectly true, though it was Raffles alone who had kept the one open, and enabled me to propitiate the other in moments of emergency.

"Well?"

"Well, pay in this bundle of notes this afternoon, and say you have had a great week at Liverpool and Lincoln; then ask them if they can do with your silver while you run over to Paris for a merry Easter. I should tell them it's rather heavy—a lot of old family stuff that you've a good mind to leave with them till you marry and settle down."

I winced at this, but consented to the rest after a moment's consideration. After all, and for more reasons that I need enumerate, it was a plausible tale enough. And Raffles had no banker; it was quite impossible for him to explain, across any single counter, the large sums of hard cash which did sometimes fall into his hands; and it might well be that he had nursed my small account in view of the very quandary which had now arisen. On all grounds, it was impossible for me to refuse him, and I am still glad to remember that my assent was given, on the whole, ungrudgingly.

"But when will the chest be ready for me I merely asked, as I stuffed the notes into my cigarette case. "And how are we to get it out of this, in banking hours, without attracting any amount of attention at this end?"

Raffles gave me an approving nod.

"I'm glad to see you spot the crux so quickly, Bunny. I have thought of your taking it round to your place first, under cloud of night; but we are bound to be seen even so, and on the whole it would look far less suspicious in broad daylight. It will take you some twelve or fifteen minutes to drive to your bank in a growler, so if you are here with one at a quarter to ten to-morrow morning, that will exactly meet the case. But you must have a hansom this minute if you mean to prepare the way with those notes this afternoon!"

It was only too like the Raffles of those days to dismiss a subject and myself in the same breath, with a sudden nod, and a brief grasp of the hand he was already holding out for mine. I had a great mind to take another of his cigarettes instead, for there were one or two points on which he had carefully omitted to enlighten me. Thus, I had still to learn the bare direction of his journey; and it was all that I could do to drag it from him as I stood buttoning my coat and gloves.

"Scotland," he vouchsafed at last.

"At Easter," I remarked.

"To learn the language," he explained. "I have no tongue but my own, you see, but I try to make up for it by cultivating every shade of that. Some of them have come in useful even to your knowledge, Bunny: what price my Cockney that night in St. John's Wood? I can keep up my end in stage Irish, real Devonshire, very fair Norfolk, and three distinct Yorkshire dialects. But my good Galloway Scots might be better, and I mean to make it so."

"You still haven't told me where to write to you."

"I'll write to you first, Bunny."

"At least let me see you off," I urged at the door. "I promise not to look at your ticket if you tell me the train!"

"The eleven-fifty from Euston."

"Then I'll be with you by quarter to ten."

And I left him without further parley, reading his impatience in his face. Everything, to be sure, seemed clear enough without that fuller discussion which I loved and Raffles hated. Yet I thought we might at least have dined together, and in my heart I felt just the least bit hurt, until it occurred to me as I drove to count the notes in my cigarette case. Resentment was impossible after that. The sum ran well into three figures, and it was plain that Raffles meant me to have a good time in his absence. So I told his lie with unction at my bank, and made due arrangements for the reception of his chest next morning. Then I repaired to our club, hoping he would drop in, and that we might dine together after all. In that I was disappointed. It was nothing, however, to the disappointment awaiting me at the Albany, when I arrived in my four-wheeler at the appointed hour next morning.

"Mr. Raffles 'as gawn, sir," said the porter, with a note of reproach in his confidential undertone. The man was a favorite with Raffles, who used him and tipped him with consummate tact, and he knew me only less well.

"Gone!" I echoed aghast. "Where on earth to?"

"Scotland, sir."

"Already?"

"By the eleven-fifty lawst night"

"Last night! I thought he meant eleven-fifty this morning!"

"He knew you did, sir, when you never came, and he told me to tell you there was no such train."

I could have rent my garments in mortification and annoyance with myself and Raffles. It was as much his fault as mine. But for his indecent haste in getting rid of me, his characteristic abruptness at the end, there would have been no misunderstanding or mistake.

"Any other message?" I inquired morosely.

"Only about the box, sir. Mr. Raffles said as you was goin' to take chawge of it time he's away, and I've a friend ready to lend a 'and in getting it on the cab. It's a rare 'eavy 'un, but Mr. Raffles an' me could lift it all right between us, so I dessay me an' my friend can."

For my own part, I must confess that its weight concerned me less than the vast size of that infernal chest, as I drove with it past club and park at ten o'clock in the morning. Sit as far back as I might in the four-wheeler, I could conceal neither myself nor my connection with the huge iron-clamped case upon the roof: in my heated imagination its wood was glass through which all the world could see the guilty contents. Once an officious constable held up the traffic at our approach, and for a moment I put a blood-curdling construction upon the simple ceremony. Low boys shouted after us—or if it was not after us, I thought it was—and that their cry was "Stop thief!" Enough said of one of the most unpleasant cab-drives I ever had in my life. Horresco referens.

At the bank, however, thanks to the foresight and liberality of Raffles, all was smooth water. I paid my cabman handsomely, gave a florin to the stout fellow in livery whom he helped with the chest, and could have pressed gold upon the genial clerk who laughed like a gentleman at my jokes about the Liverpool winners and the latest betting on the Family Plate. I was only disconcerted when he informed me that the bank gave no receipts for deposits of this nature. I am now aware that few London banks do. But it is pleasing to believe that at the time I looked—what I felt—as though all I valued upon earth were in jeopardy.

I should have got through the rest of that day happily enough, such was the load off my mind and hands, but for an extraordinary and most disconcerting note received late at night from Raffles himself. He was a man who telegraphed freely, but seldom wrote a letter. Sometimes, however, he sent a scribbled line by special messenger; and overnight, evidently in the train, he had scribbled this one to post in the small hours at Crewe:

"'Ware Prince of Professors! He was in the offing when I left. If slightest cause for uneasiness about bank, withdraw at once and keep in own rooms Like good chap,

"A. J. R.

"P. 8.—Other reasons, as you shall hear."

There was a nice nightcap for a puzzled head! I had made rather an evening of it, what with increase of funds and decrease of anxiety, but this cryptic admonition spoiled the remainder of my night. It had arrived by a late post, and I only wished that I had left it all night in my letter-box. What exactly did it mean? And what exactly must I do? These were questions that confronted me with fresh force in the morning.

The news of Crawshay did not surprise me. I was quite sure that Raffles had been given good reason to bear him in mind before his journey, even if he had not again beheld the ruffian in the flesh. That ruffian and that journey might be more intimately connected than I had yet supposed. Raffles never told me all. Yet the solid fact held good—held better than ever—that I had seen his plunder safely planted in my bank. Crawshay himself could not follow it there. I was certain he had not followed my cab: in the acute self-consciousness induced by that abominable drive, I should have known it in my bones if he had. I thought of the porter's friend who had helped me with the chest. No, I remember him as well as I remembered Crawshay; they were quite different types.

To remove that vile box from the bank, on top of another cab, with no stronger pretext and no further instructions, was not to be thought of for a moment. Yet I did think of it, for hours. I was always anxious to do my part by Raffles; he had done more than his by me, not once or twice, to-day or yesterday, but again and again from the very first. I need not state the obvious reasons I had for fighting shy of the personal custody of his accursed chest. Yet he had run worse risks for me, and I wanted him to learn that he, too, could depend on a devotion not unworthy of his own.

In my dilemma I did what I have often done when at a loss for light and leading. I took hardly any lunch, but went to Northumberland Avenue and had a Turkish bath instead. I know nothing so cleansing to mind as well as body, nothing better calculated to put the finest possible edge on such judgment as one may happen to possess. Even Raffles, without an ounce to lose or a nerve to soothe, used to own a sensuous appreciation of the peace of mind and person to be gained in this fashion when all others failed. For me, the fun began before the boots were off one's feet; the muffled footfalls, the thin sound of the fountain, even the spent swathed forms upon the couches, and the whole clean, warm, idle atmosphere, were so much unction to my simpler soul. The half-hour in the hot-rooms I used to count but a strenuous step to a divine lassitude of limb and accompanying exaltation of intellect. And yet—and yet—it was in the hottest room of all, in a temperature of 270ø Fahrenheit, that the bolt fell from the Pall Mall Gazette which I had bought outside the bath.

I was turning over the hot, crisp pages, and positively revelling in my fiery furnace, when the following headlines and leaded paragraphs leapt to my eye with the force of a veritable blow:

BANK ROBBERS IN THE WEST END—
DARING AND MYSTERIOUS CRIME

An audacious burglary and dastardly assault have been committed on the premises of the City and Suburban Bank in Sloane Street, W. From the details so far to hand, the robbery appears to have been deliberately planned and adroitly executed in the early hours of this morning.

A night watchman named Fawcett states that between one and two o'clock he heard a slight noise in the neighborhood of the lower strong-room, used as a repository for the plate and other possessions of various customers of the bank. Going down to investigate, he was instantly attacked by a powerful ruffian, who succeeded in felling him to the ground before an alarm could be raised.

Fawcett is unable to furnish any description of his assailant or assailants, but is of opinion that more than one were engaged in the commission of the crime. When the unfortunate man recovered consciousness, no trace of the thieves remained, with the exception of a single candle which had been left burning on
the flags of the corridor. The strong-room, however, had been opened, and it is feared the raid on the chests of plate and other valuables may prove to have been only too successful, in view of the Easter exodus, which the thieves had evidently taken into account. The ordinary banking chambers were not even
visited; entry and exit are believed to have been effected through the coal cellar, which is also situated in the basement. Up to the present the police have effected no arrest.

I sat practically paralyzed by this appalling news; and I swear that, even in that incredible temperature, it was a cold perspiration in which I sweltered from head to heel. Crawshay, of course! Crawshay once more upon the track of Raffles and his ill-gotten gains! And once more I blamed Raffles himself: his warning had come too late: he should have wired to me at once not to take the box to the bank at all. He was a madman ever to have invested in so obvious and obtrusive a receptacle for treasure. It would serve Raffles right if that and no other was the box which had been broken into by the thieves.

Yet, when I considered the character of his treasure, I fairly shuddered in my sweat. It was a hoard of criminal relics. Suppose his chest had indeed been rifled, and emptied of every silver thing but one; that one remaining piece of silver, seen of men, was quite enough to cast Raffles into the outer darkness of penal servitude! And Crawshay was capable of it—of perceiving the insidious revenge—of taking it without compunction or remorse.

There was only one course for me. I must follow my instructions to the letter and recover the chest at all hazards, or be taken myself in the attempt. If only Raffles had left me some address, to which I could have wired some word of warning! But it was no use thinking of that; for the rest there was time enough up to four o'clock, and as yet it was not three. I determined to go through with my bath and make the most of it. Might it not be my last for years?

But I was past enjoying even a Turkish bath. I had not the patience for a proper shampoo, or sufficient spirit for the plunge. I weighed myself automatically, for that was a matter near my heart; but I forgot to give my man his sixpence until the reproachful intonation of his adieu recalled me to myself. And my couch in the cooling gallery—my favorite couch, in my favorite corner, which I had secured with gusto on coming in—it was a bed of thorns, with hideous visions of a plank-bed to follow!

I ought to be able to add that I heard the burglary discussed on adjacent couches before I left I certainly listened for it, and was rather disappointed more than once when I had held my breath in vain. But this is the unvarnished record of an odious hour, and it passed without further aggravation from without; only, as I drove to Sloane Street, the news was on all the posters, and on one I read of "a clew" which spelt for me a doom I was grimly resolved to share.

Already there was something in the nature of a "run" up on the Sloane Street branch of the City and Suburban. A cab drove away with a chest of reasonable dimensions as mine drove up, while in the bank itself a lady was making a painful scene. As for the genial clerk who had roared at my jokes the day before, he was mercifully in no mood for any more, but, on the contrary, quite rude to me at sight.

"I've been expecting you all the afternoon," said he. "You needn't look so pale."

"Is it safe?"

"That Noah's Ark of yours? Yes, so I hear; they'd just got to it when they were interrupted, and they never went back again."

"Then it wasn't even opened?"

"Only just begun on, I believe."

"Thank God!"

"You may; we don't," growled the clerk. "The manager says he believes your chest was at the bottom of it all."

"How could it be?" I asked uneasily.

"By being seen on the cab a mile off, and followed," said the clerk.

"Does the manager want to see me?" I asked boldly.

"Not unless you want to see him," was the blunt reply. "He's been at it with others all. the afternoon, and they haven't all. got off as cheap as you."

"Then my silver shall not embarrass you any longer," said I grandly. "I meant to leave it if it was all. right, but after all. you have said I certainly shall not. Let your man or men bring up the chest at once. I dare say they also have been 'at it with others all. the afternoon,' but I shall make this worth their while."

I did not mind driving through the streets with the thing this time. My present relief was too overwhelming as yet to admit of pangs and fears for the immediate future. No summer sun had ever shone more brightly than that rather watery one of early April. There was a green-and-gold dust of buds and shoots on the trees as we passed the park. I felt greater things sprouting in my heart. Hansoms passed with schoolboys just home for the Easter holidays, four-wheelers outward bound, with bicycles and perambulators atop; none that rode in them were half so happy as I, with the great load on my cab, but the greater one off my heart.

At Mount Street it just went into the lift; that was a stroke of luck; and the lift-man and I between us carried it into my flat. It seemed a featherweight to me now. I felt a Samson in the exaltation of that hour. And I will not say what my first act was when I found myself alone with my white elephant in the middle of the room; enough that the siphon was still doing its work when the glass slipped through my fingers to the floor.

"Bunny!"

It was Raffles. Yet for a moment I looked about me quite in vain. He was not at the window; he was not at the open door. And yet Raffles it had been, or at all. events his voice, and that bubbling over with fun and satisfaction, be his body where it might. In the end I dropped my eyes, and there was his living face in the middle of the lid of the chest, like that of the saint upon its charger.

But Raffles was alive, Raffles was laughing as though his vocal cords would snap—there was neither tragedy nor illusion in the apparition of Raffles. A life-size Jack-in-the-box, he had thrust his head through a lid within the lid, cut by himself between the two iron bands that ran round the chest like the straps of a portmanteau. He must have been busy at it when I found him pretending to pack, if not far into that night, for it was a very perfect piece of work; and even as I stared without a word, and he crouched laughing in my face, an arm came squeezing out, keys in hand; one was turned in either of the two great padlocks, the whole lid lifted, and out stepped Raffles like the conjurer he was.

"So you were the burglar!" I exclaimed at last. "Well, I am just as glad I didn't know."

He had wrung my hand already, but at this he fairly mangled it in his.

"You dear little brick," he cried, "that's the one thing of all. things I longed to hear you say! How could you have behaved as you've done if you had known? How could any living man? How could you have acted, as the polar star of all. the stages could not have acted in your place? Remember that I have heard a lot, and as good as seen as much as I've heard. Bunny, I don't know where you were greatest: at the Albany, here, or at your bank!"

"I don't know where I was most miserable," I rejoined, beginning to see the matter in a less perfervid light. "I know you don't credit me with much finesse, but I would undertake to be in the secret and to do quite as well; the only difference would be in my own peace of mind, which, of course, doesn't count."

But Raffles wagged away with his most charming and disarming smile; he was in old clothes, rather tattered and torn, and more than a little grimy as to the face and hands, but, on the surface, wonderfully little the worse for his experience. And, as I say, his smile was the smile of the Raffles I loved best.

"You would have done your damnedest, Bunny! There is no limit to your heroism; but you forget the human equation in the pluckiest of the plucky. I couldn't afford to forget it, Bunny; I couldn't afford to give a point away. Don't talk as though I hadn't trusted you! I trusted my very life to your loyal tenacity. What do you suppose would have happened to me if you had let me rip in that strong-room? Do you think I would ever have crept out and given myself up? Yes, I'll have a peg for once; the beauty of all. laws is in the breaking, even of the kind we make unto ourselves."

I had a Sullivan for him, too; and in another minute he was spread out on my sofa, stretching his cramped limbs with infinite gusto, a cigarette between his fingers, a yellow bumper at hand on the chest of his triumph and my tribulation.

"Never mind when it occurred to me, Bunny; as a matter of fact, it was only the other day, when I had decided to go away for the real reasons I have already given you. I may have made more of them to you than I do in my own mind, but at all. events they exist. And I really did want the telephone and the electric light."

"But where did you stow the silver before you went?"

"Nowhere; it was my luggage—a portmanteau, cricket-bag, and suit-case full of very little else—and by the same token I left the lot at Euston, and one of us must fetch them this evening."

"I can do that," said I. "But did you really go all. the way to Crewe?"

"Didn't you get my note? I went all. the way to Crewe to post you those few lines, my dear Bunny! It's no use taking trouble if you don't take trouble enough; I wanted you to show the proper set of faces at the bank and elsewhere, and I know you did. Besides, there was an up-train four minutes after mine got in. I simply posted my letter in Crewe station, and changed from one train to the other."

"At two in the morning!"

"Nearer three, Bunny. It was after seven when I slung in with the Daily Mail. The milk had beaten me by a short can. But even so I had two very good hours before you were due."

"And to think," I murmured, "how you deceived me there!"

"With your own assistance," said Raffles laughing. "If you had looked it up you would have seen there was no such train in the morning, and I never said there was. But I meant you to be deceived, Bunny, and I won't say I didn't—it was all. for the sake of the side! Well, when you carted me away with such laudable despatch, I had rather an uncomfortable half-hour, but that was all. just then. I had my candle, I had matches, and lots to read. It was quite nice in that strong-room until a very unpleasant incident occurred."

"Do tell me, my dear fellow!"

"I must have another Sullivan—thank you—and a match. The unpleasant incident was steps outside and a key in the lock! I was disporting myself on the lid of the trunk at the time. I had barely time to knock out my light and slip down behind it. Luckily it was only another box of sorts; a jewel-case, to be more precise; you shall see the contents in a moment. The Easter exodus has done me even better than I dared to hope."

His words reminded me of the Pall Mall Gazette, which I had brought in my pocket from the Turkish bath. I fished it out, all. wrinkled and bloated by the heat of the hottest room, and handed it to Raffles with my thumb upon the leaded paragraphs.

"Delightful!" said he when he had read them. "More thieves than one, and the coal-cellar of all. places as a way in! I certainly tried to give it that appearance. I left enough candle-grease there to make those coals burn bravely. But it looked up into a blind backyard, Bunny, and a boy of eight couldn't have squeezed through the trap. Long may that theory keep them happy at Scotland Yard!"

"But what about the fellow you knocked out?" I asked. "That was not like you, Raffles."

Raffles blew pensive rings as he lay back on my sofa, his black hair tumbled on the cushion, his pale profile as clear and sharp against the light as though slashed out with the scissors.

"I know it wasn't, Bunny," he said regretfully. "But things like that, as the poet will tell you, are really inseparable from victories like mine. It had taken me a couple of hours to break out of that strong-room; I was devoting a third to the harmless task of simulating the appearance of having broken in; and it was then I heard the fellow's stealthy step. Some might have stood their ground and killed him; more would have bolted into a worse corner than they were in already. I left my candle where it was, crept to meet the poor devil, flattened myself against the wall, and let him have it as he passed. I acknowledge the foul blow, but here's evidence that it was mercifully struck. The victim has already told his tale."

As he drained his glass, but shook his head when I wished to replenish it, Raffles showed me the flask which he had carried in his pocket: it was still nearly full; and I found that he had otherwise provisioned himself over the holidays. On either Easter Day or Bank Holiday, had I failed him, it had been his intention to make the best escape he could. But the risk must have been enormous, and it filled my glowing skin to think that he had not relied on me in vain.

As for his gleanings from such jewel-cases as were spending the Easter recess in the strong-room of my bank, without going into rhapsodies or even particulars on the point,) I may mention that they realized enough for me to join Raffles on his deferred holiday in Scotland, besides enabling him to play more regularly for Middlesex in the ensuing summer than had been the case for several seasons. In fine, this particular exploit entirely justified itself in my eyes, in spite of the superfluous (but invariable) secretiveness which I could seldom help resenting in my heart I never thought less of it than in the present instance; and my one mild reproach was on the subject of the phantom Crawshay.

"You let me think he was in the air again," I said. "But it wouldn't surprise me to find that you had never heard of him since the day of his escape through your window."

"I never even thought of him, Bunny, until you came to see me the day before yesterday, and put him into my head with your first words. The whole point was to make you as genuinely anxious about the plate as you must have seemed all. along the line."

"Of course I see your point," I rejoined; "but mine is that you labored it. You needn't have written me a downright lie about the fellow."

"Nor did I, Bunny."

"Not about the 'prince of professors' being 'in the offing' when you left?"

"My dear Bunny, but so he was!" cried Raffles. "Time was when I was none too pure an amateur. But after this I take leave to consider myself a professor of the professors. And I should like to see one more capable of skippering their side!"

The Rest Cure

I had not seen Raffles for a month or more, and I was sadly in need of his advice. My life was being made a burden to me by a wretch who had obtained a bill of sale over the furniture in Mount Street, and it was only by living elsewhere that I could keep the vulpine villain from my door. This cost ready money, and my balance at the bank was sorely in need of another lift from Raffles. Yet, had he been in my shoes, he could not have vanished more effectually than he had done, both from the face of the town and from the ken of all. who knew him.

It was late in August; he never played first-class cricket after July, when, a scholastic understudy took his place in the Middlesex eleven. And in vain did I scour my Field and my Sportsman for the country-house matches with which he wilfully preferred to wind up the season; the matches were there, but never the magic name of A. J. Raffles. Nothing was known of him at the Albany; he had left no instructions about his letters, either there or at the club. I began to fear that some evil had overtaken him. I scanned the features of captured criminals in the illustrated Sunday papers; on each occasion I breathed again; nor was anything worthy of Raffles going on. I will not deny that I was less anxious on his account than on my own. But it was a double relief to me when he gave a first characteristic sign of life.

I had called at the Albany for the fiftieth time, and returned to Piccadilly in my usual despair, when a street sloucher sidled up to me in furtive fashion and inquired if my name was what it is.

"'Cause this 'ere's for you," he rejoined to my affirmative, and with that I felt a crumpled note in my palm.

It was from Raffles. I smoothed out the twisted scrap of paper, and on it were just a couple of lines in pencil:

"Meet me in Holland Walk at dark to-night. Walk up and down till I come. A. J. R."

That was all.! Not another syllable after all. these weeks, and the few words scribbled in a wild caricature of his scholarly and dainty hand! I was no longer to be alarmed by this sort of thing; it was all. so like the Raffles I loved least; and to add to my indignation, when at length I looked up from the mysterious missive, the equally mysterious messenger had disappeared in a manner worthy of the whole affair. He was, however, the first creature I espied under the tattered trees of Holland Walk that evening.

"Seen 'im yet?" he inquired confidentially, blowing a vile cloud from his horrid pipe.

"No, I haven't; and I want to know where you've seen him," I replied sternly. "Why did you run away like that the moment you had given me his note?"

"Orders, orders," was the reply. "I ain't such a juggins as to go agen a toff as makes it worf while to do as I'm bid an' 'old me tongue."

"And who may you be?" I asked jealously. "And what are you to Mr. Raffles?"

"You silly ass, Bunny, don't tell all. Kensington that I'm in town!" replied my tatterdemalion, shooting up and smoothing out into a merely shabby Raffles. "Here, take my arm—I'm not so beastly as I look. But neither am I in town, nor in England, nor yet on the face of the earth, for all. that's known of me to a single soul but you."

"Then where are you," I asked, "between ourselves?"

"I've taken a house near here for the holidays, where I'm going in for a Rest Cure of my own description. Why? Oh, for lots of reasons, my dear Bunny; among others, I have long had a wish to grow my own beard; under the next lamppost you will agree that it's training on very nicely. Then, you mayn't know it, but there's a canny man at Scotland Yard who has had a quiet eye on me longer than I like. I thought it about time to have an eye on him, and I stared him in the face outside the Albany this very morning. That was when I saw you go in, and scribbled a line to give you when you came out. If he had caught us talking he would have spotted me at once."

"So you are lying low out here!"

"I prefer to call it my Rest Cure," returned Raffles, "and it's really nothing else. I've got a furnished house at a time when no one else would have dreamed of taking one in town; and my very neighbors don't know I'm there, though I'm bound to say there are hardly any of them at home. I don't keep a servant, and do everything for myself. It's the next best fun to a desert island. Not that I make much work, for I'm really resting, but I haven't done so much solid reading for years. Rather a joke, Bunny: the man whose house I've taken is one of her Majesty's inspectors of prisons, and his study's a storehouse of criminology. It has been quite amusing to lie on one's back and have a good look at one's self as others fondly imagine they see one."

"But surely you get some exercise?" I asked; for he was leading me at a good rate through the leafy byways of Camp den Hill; and his step was as springy and as light as ever.

"The best exercise I ever had in my life," said Raffles; "and you would never live to guess what it is. It's one of the reasons why I went in for this seedy kit. I follow cabs. Yes, Bunny, I turn out about dusk and meet the expresses at Euston or King's Cross; that is, of course, I loaf outside and pick my cab, and often run my three or four miles for a bob or less. And it not only keeps you in the very pink: if you're good they let you carry the trunks up-stairs; and I've taken notes from the inside of more than one commodious residence which will come in useful in the autumn. In fact, Bunny, what with these new Rowton houses, my beard, and my otherwise well-spent holiday, I hope to have quite a good autumn season before the erratic Raffles turns up in town."

I felt it high time to wedge in a word about my own far less satisfactory affairs. But it was not necessary for me to recount half my troubles. Raffles could be as full of himself as many a worse man, and I did not like his society the less for these human outpourings. They had rather the effect of putting me on better terms with myself, through bringing him down to my level for the time being. But his egoism was not even skin-deep; it was rather a cloak, which

Raffles could cast off quicker than any man I ever knew, as he did not fail to show me now.

"Why, Bunny, this is the very thing!" he cried. "You must come and stay with me, and we'll lie low side by side. Only remember it really is a Rest Cure. I want to keep literally as quiet as I was without you. What do you say to forming ourselves at once into a practically Silent Order? You agree? Very well, then, here's the street and that's the house."

It was ever such a quiet little street, turning out of one of those which climb right over the pleasant hill. One side was monopolized by the garden wall of an ugly but enviable mansion standing in its own ground; opposite were a solid file of smaller but taller houses; on neither side were there many windows alight, nor a solitary soul on the pavement or in the road. Raffles led the way to one of the small tall houses. It stood immediately behind a lamppost, and I could not but notice that a love-lock of Virginia creeper was trailing almost to the step, and that the bow-window on the ground floor was closely shuttered. Raffles admitted himself with his latch-key, and I squeezed past him into a very narrow hall. I did not hear him shut the door, but we were no longer in the lamplight, and he pushed softly past me in his turn.

"I'll get a light," he muttered as he went; but to let him pass I had leaned against some electric switches, and while 'his back was turned I tried one of these without thinking. In an instant hall and staircase were flooded with light; in another Raffles was upon me in a fury, and, all. was dark once more. He had not said a word, but I heard him breathing through his teeth.

Nor was there anything to tell me now. The mere flash of electric light upon a hail of chaos and uncarpeted stairs, and on the face of Raffles as he sprang to switch it off, had been enough even for me.

"So this is how you have taken the house," said I in his own undertone.

"'Taken' is good; 'taken' is beautiful!"

"Did you think I'd done it through an agent?" he snarled. "Upon my word, Bunny, I did you the credit of supposing you saw the joke all. the time!"

"Why shouldn't you take a house," I asked, "and pay for it?"

"Why should I," he retorted, "within three miles of the Albany? Besides, I should have had no peace; and I meant every word I said about my Rest Cure."

"You are actually staying in a house where you've broken in to steal?"

"Not to steal, Bunny! I haven't stolen a thing. But staying here I certainly am, and having the most complete rest a busy man could wish."

"There'll be no rest for me!"

Raffles laughed as he struck a match. I had followed him into what would have been the back drawing-room in the ordinary little London house; the inspector of prisons had converted it into a separate study by filling the folding doors with book-shelves, which I scanned at once for the congenial works of which Raffles had spoken. I was not able to carry my examination very far. Raffles had lighted a candle, stuck (by its own grease) in the crown of an opera hat, which he opened the moment the wick caught. The light thus struck the ceiling in an oval shaft, which left the rest of the room almost as dark as it had been before.

"Sorry, Bunny!" said Raffles, sitting on one pedestal of a desk from which the top had been removed, and setting his makeshift lantern on the other. "In broad daylight, when it can't be spotted from the outside, you shall have as much artificial light as you like. If you want to do some writing, that's the top of the desk on end against the mantlepiece. You'll never have a better chance so far as interruption goes. But no midnight oil or electricity! You observe that their last care was to fix up these shutters; they appear to have taken the top off the desk to get at 'em without standing on it; but the beastly things wouldn't go all. the way up, and the strip they leave would give us away to the backs of the other houses if we lit up after dark. Mind that telephone! If you touch the receiver they will know at the exchange that the house is not empty, and I wouldn't put it past the colonel to have told them exactly how long he was going to be away. He's pretty particular: look at the strips of paper to keep the dust off his precious books!"

"Is he a colonel?" I asked, perceiving that Raffles referred to the absentee householder.

"Of sappers," he replied, "and a V.C. into the bargain, confound him! Got it at Rorke's Drift; prison governor or inspector ever since; favorite recreation, what do you think? Revolver shooting! You can read all. about him in his own Who's Who. A devil of a chap to tackle, Bunny, when he's at home!"

"And where is he now?" I asked uneasily. And do you know he isn't on his way home?"

"Switzerland," replied Raffles, chuckling; "he wrote one too many labels, and was considerate enough to leave it behind for our guidance. Well, no one ever comes back from Switzerland at the beginning of September, you know; and nobody ever thinks of coming back before the servants. When they turn up they won't get in. I keep the latch jammed, but the servants will think it's jammed itself, and while they're gone for the locksmith we shall walk out like gentlemen—if we haven't done so already."

"As you walked in, I suppose?"

Raffles shook his head in the dim light to which my sight was growing inured.

"No, Bunny, I regret to say I came in through the dormer window. They were painting next door but one. I never did like ladder work, but it takes less time than in picking a lock in the broad light of a street lamp."

"So they left you a latch-key as well as everything else!"

"No, Bunny. I was just able to make that for myself. I am playing at 'Robinson Crusoe,' not 'The Swiss Family Robinson.' And now, my dear Friday, if you will kindly take off those boots, we can explore the island before we turn in for the night."

The stairs were very steep and narrow, and they creaked alarmingly as Raffles led the way up, with the single candle in the crown of the colonel's hat. He blew it out before we reached the half-landing, where a naked window stared upon the backs of the houses in the next road, but lit it again at the drawing-room door. I just peeped in upon a semi-grand swathed in white and a row of water colors mounted in gold. An excellent bathroom broke our journey to the second floor.

"I'll have one to-night," said I, taking heart of a luxury unknown in my last sordid sanctuary.

"You'll do no such thing," snapped Raffles. "Have the goodness to remember that our island is one of a group inhabited by hostile tribes. You can fill the bath quietly if you try, but it empties under the study window, and makes the very devil of a noise about it. No, Bunny, I bale out every drop and pour it away through the scullery sink, so you will kindly consult me before you turn a tap. Here's your room; hold the light outside while I draw the curtains; it's the old chap's dressing-room. Now you can bring the glim. How's that for a jolly wardrobe? And look at his coats on their cross-trees inside: dapper old dog, shouldn't you say? Mark the boots on the shelf above, and the little brass rail for his ties! Didn't I tell you he was particular? And wouldn't he simply love to catch us at his kit?"

"Let's only hope it would give him an apoplexy," said I shuddering.

"I shouldn't build on it," replied Raffles. "That's a big man's trouble, and neither you nor I could get into the old chap's clothes. But come into the best bedroom, Bunny. You won't think me selfish if I don't give it up to you? Look at this, my boy, look at this! It's the only one I use in all. the house."

I had followed him into a good room, with ample windows closely curtained, and he had switched on the light in a hanging lamp at the bedside. The rays fell from a thick green funnel in a plateful of strong light upon a table deep in books. I noticed several volumes of the "Invasion of the Crimea."

"That's where I rest the body and exercise the brain," said Raffles. "I have long wanted to read my Kinglake from A to Z, and I manage about a volume a night. There's a style for you, Bunny! I love the punctilious thoroughness of the whole thing; one can understand its appeal to our careful colonel. His name, did you say? Crutchley, Bunny—Colonel Crutchley, R.E., V.C."

"We'd put his valor to the test!" said I, feeling more valiant myself after our tour of inspection.

"Not so loud on the stairs," whispered Raffles. "There's only one door between us and—"

Raffles stood still at my feet, and well he might! A deafening double knock had resounded through the empty house; and to add to the utter horror of the moment, Raffles instantly blew out the light. I heard my heart pounding. Neither of us breathed. We were on our way down to the first landing, and for a moment we stood like mice; then Raffles heaved a deep sigh, and in the depths I heard the gate swing home.

"Only the postman, Bunny! He will come now and again, though they have obviously left instructions at the post-office. I hope the old colonel will let them have it when he gets back. I confess it gave me a turn."

"Turn!" I gasped. "I must have a drink, if I die for it."

"My dear Bunny, that's no part of my Rest Cure."

"Then good-by! I can't stand it; feel my forehead; listen to my heart! Crusoe found a footprint, but he never heard a double-knock at the street door!"

"'Better live in the midst of alarms,'" quoted Raffles, "'than dwell in this horrible place.' I must confess we get it both ways, Bunny. Yet I've nothing but tea in the house."

"And where do you make that? Aren't you afraid of smoke?"

"There's a gas-stove in the dining-room."

"But surely to goodness," I cried, "there's a cellar lower down!"

"My dear, good Bunny," said Raffles, "I've told you already that I didn't come in here on business. I came in for the Cure. Not a penny will these people be the worse, except for their washing and their electric light, and I mean to leave enough to cover both items."

"Then," said I, "since Brutus is such a very honorable man, we will borrow a bottle from the cellar, and replace it before we go."

Raffles slapped me softly on the back, and I knew that I had gained my point. It was often the case when I had the presence of heart and mind to stand up to him. But never was little victory of mine quite so grateful as this. Certainly it was a very small cellar, indeed a mere cupboard under the kitchen stairs, with a most ridiculous lock. Nor was this cupboard overstocked with wine. But I made out a jar of whiskey, a shelf of Zeltinger, another of claret, and a short one at the top which presented a little battery of golden-leafed necks and corks. Raffles set his hand no lower. He examined the labels while I held folded hat and naked light.

"Mumm, '84!" he whispered. "G. H. Mumm, and A.D. 1884! I am no wine-bibber, Bunny, as you know, but I hope you appreciate the specifications as I do. It looks to me like the only bottle, the last of its case, and it does seem a bit of a shame; but more shame for the miser who hoards in his cellar what was meant for mankind! Come, Bunny, lead the way. This baby is worth nursing. It would break my heart if anything happened to it now!"

So we celebrated my first night in the furnished house; and I slept beyond belief, slept as I never was to sleep there again. But it was strange to hear the milkman in the early morning, and the postman knocking his way along the street an hour later, and to be passed over by one destroying angel after another. I had come down early enough, and watched through the drawing-room blind the cleansing of all. the steps in the street but ours. Yet Raffles had evidently been up some time; the house seemed far purer than overnight as though he had managed to air it room by room; and from the one with the gas-stove there came a frizzling sound that fattened the heart.

I only would I had the pen to do justice to the week I spent in-doors on Campden Hill! It might make amusing reading; the reality for me was far removed from the realm of amusement. Not that I was denied many a laugh of suppressed heartiness when Raffles and I were together. But half our time we very literally saw nothing of each other. I need not say whose fault that was. He would be quiet; he was in ridiculous and offensive earnest about his egregious

Cure. Kinglake he would read by the hour together, day and night, by the hanging lamp, lying up-stairs on the best bed. There was daylight enough for me in the drawing-room below; and there I would sit immersed in criminous tomes weakly fascinated until I shivered and shook in my stocking soles. Often I longed to do something hysterically desperate, to rouse Raffles and bring the street about our ears; once I did bring him about mine by striking a single note on the piano, with the soft pedal down. His neglect of me seemed wanton at the time. I have long realized that he was only wise to maintain silence at the expense of perilous amenities, and as fully justified in those secret and solitary sorties which made bad blood in my veins. He was far cleverer than I at getting in and out; but even had I been his match for stealth and wariness, my company would have doubled every risk. I admit now that he treated me with quite as much sympathy as common caution would permit. But at the time I took it so badly as to plan a small revenge.

What with his flourishing beard and the increasing shabbiness of the only suit he had brought with him to the house, there was no denying that Raffles had now the advantage of a permanent disguise. That was another of his excuses for leaving me as he did, and it was the one I was determined to remove. On a morning, therefore, when I awoke to find him flown again, I proceeded to execute a plan which I had already matured in my mind. Colonel Crutchley was a married man; there were no signs of children in the house; on the other hand, there was much evidence that the wife was a woman of fashion. Her dresses overflowed the wardrobe and her room; large, flat, cardboard boxes were to be found in every corner of the upper floors. She was a tall woman; I was not too tall a man. Like Raffles, I had not shaved on Campden Hill. That morning, however, I did my best with a very fair razor which the colonel had left behind in my room; then I turned out the lady's wardrobe and the cardboard boxes, and took my choice.

I have fair hair, and at the time it was rather long. With a pair of Mrs. Crutchley's tongs and a discarded hair-net, I was able to produce an almost immodest fringe. A big black hat with a wintry feather completed a headdress as unseasonable as my skating skirt and feather boa; of course, the good lady had all. her summer frocks away with her in Switzerland. This was all. the more annoying from the fact that we were having a very warm September; so I was not sorry to hear Raffles return as I was busy adding a layer of powder to my heated countenance. I listened a moment on the landing, but as he went into the study I determined to complete my toilet in every detail. My idea was first to give him the fright he deserved, and secondly to show him that I was quite as fit to move abroad as he. It was, however, I confess, a pair of the colonel's gloves that I was buttoning as I slipped down to the study even more quietly than usual. The electric light was on, as it generally was by day, and under it stood as formidable a figure as ever I encountered in my life of crime.

Imagine a thin but extremely wiry man, past middle age, brown and bloodless as any crabapple, but as coolly truculent and as casually alert as Raffles at his worst. It was, it could only be, the fire-eating and prison-inspecting colonel himself! He was ready for me, a revolver in his hand, taken, as I could see, from one of those locked drawers in the pedestal desk with which Raffles had refused to tamper; the drawer was open, and a bunch of keys depended from the lock. A grim smile crumpled up the parchment face, so that one eye was puckered out of sight; the other was propped open by an eyeglass, which, however, dangled on its string when I appeared.

"A woman, begad!" the warrior exclaimed. "And where's the man, you scarlet hussy?"

Not a word could I utter. But, in my horror and my amazement, I have no sort of doubt that I acted the part I had assumed in a manner I never should have approached in happier circumstances.

"Come, come, my lass," cried the old oak veteran, "I'm not going to put a bullet through you, you know! You tell me all. about it, and it'll do you more good than harm. There, I'll put the nasty thing away and—God bless me, if the brazen wench hasn't squeezed into the wife's kit!"

A squeeze it happened to have been, and in my emotion it felt more of one than ever; but his sudden discovery had not heightened the veteran's animosity against me. On the contrary, I caught a glint of humor through his gleaming glass, and he proceeded to pocket his revolver like the gentleman he was.

"Well, well, it's lucky I looked in," he continued. "I only came round on the off-chance of letters, but if I hadn't you'd have had another week in clover. Begad, though, I saw your handwriting the moment I'd got my nose inside! Now just be sensible and tell me where your good man is."

I had no man. I was alone, had broken in alone. There was not a soul in the affair (much less the house) except myself. So much I stuttered out in tones too hoarse to betray me on the spot. But the old man of the world shook a hard old head.

"Quite right not to give away your pal," said he. "But I'm not one of the marines, my dear, and you mustn't expect me to swallow all. that. Well, if you won't say, you won't, and we must just send for those who will."

In a flash I saw his fell design. The telephone directory lay open on one of the pedestals. He must have been consulting it when he heard me on the stairs; he had another look at it now; and that gave me my opportunity. With a presence of mind rare enough in me to excuse the boast, I flung myself upon the instrument in the corner and hurled it to the ground with all. my might. I was myself sent spinning into the opposite corner at the same instant. But the instrument happened to be a standard of the more elaborate pattern, and I flattered myself that I had put the delicate engine out of action for the day.

Not that my adversary took the trouble to ascertain. He was looking at me strangely in the electric light, standing intently on his guard, his right hand in the pocket where he had dropped his revolver. And I—I hardly knew it—but I caught up the first thing handy for self-defence, and was brandishing the bottle which Raffles and I had emptied in honor of my arrival on this fatal scene.

"Be shot if I don't believe you're the man himself!" cried the colonel, shaking an armed fist in my face. "You young wolf in sheep's clothing. Been at my wine, of course! Put down that bottle; down with it this instant, or I'll drill a tunnel through your middle. I thought so! Begad, sir, you shall pay for this! Don't you give me an excuse for potting you now, or I'll jump at the chance! My last bottle of '84—you miserable blackguard—you unutterable beast!"

He had browbeaten me into his own chair in his own corner; he was standing over me, empty bottle in one hand, revolver in the other, and murder itself in the purple puckers of his raging face. His language I will not even pretend to indicate: his skinny throat swelled and trembled with the monstrous volleys. He could smile at my appearance in his wife's clothes; he would have had my blood for the last bottle of his best champagne. His eyes were not hidden now; they needed no eyeglass to prop them open; large with fury, they started from the livid mask. I watched nothing else. I could not understand why they should start out as they did. I did not try. I say I watched nothing else—until I saw the face of Raffles over the unfortunate officer's shoulder.

Raffles had crept in unheard while our altercation was at its height, had watched his opportunity, and stolen on his man unobserved by either of us. While my own attention was completely engrossed, he had seized the colonel's pistol-hand and twisted it behind the colonel's back until his eyes bulged out as I have endeavored to describe. But the fighting man had some fight in him still; and scarcely had I grasped the situation when he hit out venomously behind with the bottle, which was smashed to bits on Raffles's shin. Then I threw my strength into the scale; and before many minutes we had our officer gagged and bound in his chair. But it was not one of our bloodless victories. Raffles had been cut to the bone by the broken glass; his leg bled wherever he limped; and the fierce eyes of the bound man followed the wet trail with gleams of sinister satisfaction.

I thought I had never seen a man better bound or better gagged. But the humanity seemed to have run out of Raffles with his blood. He tore up tablecloths, he cut down blind-cords, he brought the dust-sheets from the drawing-room, and multiplied every bond. The unfortunate man's legs were lashed to the legs of his chair, his arms to its arms, his thighs and back fairly welded to the leather. Either end of his own ruler protruded from his bulging cheeks—the middle was hidden by his moustache—and the gag kept in place by remorseless lashings at the back of his head. It was a spectacle I could not bear to contemplate at length, while from the first I found myself physically unable to face the ferocious gaze of those implacable eyes. But Raffles only laughed at my squeamishness, and flung a dust-sheet over man and chair; and the stark outline drove me from the room.

It was Raffles at his worst, Raffles as I never knew him before or after—a Raffles mad with pain and rage, and desperate as any other criminal in the land. Yet he had struck no brutal blow, he had uttered no disgraceful taunt, and probably not inflicted a tithe of the pain he had himself to bear. It is true that he was flagrantly in the wrong, his victim as laudably in the right. Nevertheless, granting the original sin of the situation, and given this unforeseen development, even I failed to see how Raffles could have combined greater humanity with any regard for our joint safety; and had his barbarities ended here, I for one should not have considered them an extraordinary aggravation of an otherwise minor offence. But in the broad daylight of the bathroom, which had a ground-glass window but no blind, I saw at once the serious nature of his wound and of its effect upon the man.

"It will maim me for a month," said he; "and if the V.C. comes out alive, the wound he gave may be identified with the wound I've got."

The V.C.! There, indeed, was an aggravation to one illogical mind. But to cast a moment's doubt upon the certainty of his coming out alive!

"Of course he'll come out," said I. "We must make up our minds to that."

"Did he tell you he was expecting the servants or his wife? If so, of course we must hurry up."

"No, Raffles, I'm afraid he's not expecting anybody. He told me, if he hadn't looked in for letters, we should have had the place to ourselves another week. That's the worst of it."

Raffles smiled as he secured a regular puttee of dust-sheeting. No blood was coming through.

"I don't agree, Bunny," said he. "It's quite the best of it, if you ask me."

"What, that he should die the death?"

"Why not?"

And Raffles stared me out with a hard and merciless light in his clear blue eyes—a light that chilled the blood.

"If it's a choice between his life and our liberty, you're entitled to your decision and I'm entitled to mine, and I took it before I bound him as I did," said Raffles. "I'm only sorry I took so much trouble if you're going to stay behind and put him in the way of releasing himself before he gives up the ghost. Perhaps you will go and think it over while I wash my bags and dry 'em at the gas stove. It will take me at least an hour, which will just give me time to finish the last volume of Kinglake."

Long before he was ready to go, however, I was waiting in the hall, clothed indeed, but not in a mind which I care to recall. Once or twice I peered into the dining-room where Raffles sat before the stove, without letting him hear me. He, too, was ready for the street at a moment's notice; but a steam ascended from his left leg, as he sat immersed in his red volume. Into the study I never went again; but Raffles did, to restore to its proper shelf this and every other book he had taken out and so destroy that clew to the manner of man who had made himself at home in the house. On his last visit I heard him whisk off the dust-sheet; then he waited a minute; and when he came out it was to lead the way into the open air as though the accursed house belonged to him.

"We shall be seen," I whispered at his heels. "Raffles, Raffles, there's a policeman at the corner!"

"I know him intimately," replied Raffles, turning, however, the other way. "He accosted me on Monday, when I explained that I was an old soldier of the colonel's regiment, who came in every few days to air the place and send on any odd letters. You see, I have always carried one or two about me, redirected to that address in Switzerland, and when I showed them to him it was all. right. But after that it was no use listening at the letter-box for a clear coast, was it?"

I did not answer; there was too much to exasperate in these prodigies of cunning which he could never trouble to tell me at the time. And I knew why he had kept his latest feats to himself: unwilling to trust me outside the house, he had systematically exaggerated the dangers of his own walks abroad; and when to these injuries he added the insult of a patronizing compliment on my late disguise, I again made no reply.

"What's the good of your coming with me he asked, when I had followed him across the main stream of Notting Hill.

"We may as well sink or swim together," I answered sullenly.

"Yes? Well, I'm going to swim into the provinces, have a shave on the way, buy a new kit piecemeal, including a cricket-bag (which I really want), and come limping back to the Albany with the same old strain in my bowling leg. I needn't add that I have been playing country-house cricket for the last month under an alias; it's the only decent way to do it when one's county has need of one. That's my itinerary, Bunny, but I really can't see why you should come with me."

"We may as well swing together!" I growled.

"As you will, my dear fellow," replied Raffles. "But I begin to dread your company on the drop!"

I shall hold my pen on that provincial tour. Not that I joined Raffles in any of the little enterprises with which he beguiled the breaks in our journey; our last deed in London was far too great a weight upon my soul. I could see that gallant officer in his chair, see him at every hour of the day and night, now with his indomitable eyes meeting mine ferociously, now a stark outline underneath a sheet. The vision darkened my day and gave me sleepless nights. I was with our victim in all. his agony; my mind would only leave him for that gallows of which Raffles had said true things in jest. No, I could not face so vile a death lightly, but I could meet it, somehow, better than I could endure a guilty suspense. In the watches of the second night I made up my mind to meet it halfway, that very morning, while still there might be time to save the life that we had left in jeopardy. And I got up early to tell Raffles of my resolve.

His room in the hotel where we were staying was littered with clothes and luggage new enough for any bridegroom; I lifted the locked cricket-bag, and found it heavier than a cricket-bag has any right to be. But in the bed Raffles was sleeping like an infant, his shaven self once more. And when I shook him he awoke with a smile.

"Going to confess, eh, Bunny? Well, wait a bit; the local police won't thank you for knocking them up at this hour. And I bought a late edition which you ought to see; that must be it on the floor. You have a look in the stop-press column, Bunny."

I found the place with a sunken heart, and this is what I read:

WEST-END OUTRAGE

Colonel Crutchley, R.E., V.C., has been the victim of a dastardly outrage at his residence, Peter Street, Campden Hill. Returning unexpectedly to the house, which had been left untenanted during the absence of the family abroad, it was found occupied by two ruffians, who overcame and secured the distinguished officer by the exercise of considerable violence. When discovered through the intelligence of the Kensington police, the gallant victim was gagged and bound hand and foot, and in an advanced stage of exhaustion.

"Thanks to the Kensington police," observed Raffles, as I read the last words aloud in my horror. "They can't have gone when they got my letter."

"Your letter?"

"I printed them a line while we were waiting for our train at Euston. They must have got it that night, but they can't have paid any attention to it until yesterday morning. And when they do, they take all. the credit and give me no more than you did, Bunny!"

I looked at the curly head upon the pillow, at the smiling, handsome face under the curls. And at last I understood.

"So all. the time you never meant it!"

"Slow murder? You should have known me better. A few hours' enforced Rest Cure was the worst I wished him."

"'you might have told me, Raffles!"

"That may be, Bunny, but you ought certainly to have trusted me!"

The Criminologists' Club

"But who are they, Raffles, and where's their house? There's no such club on the list in Whitaker."

"The Criminologists, my dear Bunny, are too few for a local habitation, and too select to tell their name in Gath. They are merely so many solemn students of contemporary crime, who meet and dine periodically at each other's clubs or houses."

"But why in the world should they ask us to dine with them?"

And I brandished the invitation which had brought me hotfoot to the Albany: it was from the Right Hon. the Earl of Thornaby, K.G.; and it requested the honor of my company at dinner, at Thornaby House, Park Lane, to meet the members of the Criminologists' Club. That in itself was a disturbing compliment: judge then of my dismay on learning that Raffles had been invited too!

"They have got it into their heads," said he, "that the gladiatorial element is the curse of most modern sport. They tremble especially for the professional gladiator. And they want to know whether my experience tallies with their theory."

"So they say!"

"They quote the case of a league player, sus per coll., and any number of suicides. It really is rather in my public line."

"In yours, if you like, but not in mine," said I. "No, Raffles, they've got their eye on us both, and mean to put us under the microscope, or they never would have pitched on me."

Raffles smiled on my perturbation.

"I almost wish you were right, Bunny! It would be even better fun than I mean to make it as it is. But it may console you to hear that it was I who gave them your name. I told them you were a far keener criminologist than myself. I am delighted to hear they have taken my hint, and that we are to meet at their gruesome board."

"If I accept," said I, with the austerity he deserved.

"If you don't," rejoined Raffles, "you will miss some sport after both our hearts. Think of it, Bunny! These fellows meet to wallow in all. the latest crimes; we wallow with them as though we knew more about it than themselves. Perhaps we don't, for few criminologists have a soul above murder; and I quite expect to have the privilege of lifting the discussion into our own higher walk. They shall give their morbid minds to the fine art of burgling, for a change; and while we're about it, Bunny, we may as well extract their opinion of our noble selves. As authors, as collaborators, we will sit with the flower of our critics, and find our own level in the expert eye. It will be a piquant experience, if not an invaluable one; if we are sailing too near the wind, we are sure to hear about it, and can trim our yards accordingly. Moreover, we shall get a very good dinner into the bargain, or our noble host will belie a European reputation."

"Do you know him?" I asked.

"We have a pavilion acquaintance, when it suits my lord," replied Raffles, chuckling. "But I know all. about him. He was president one year of the M.C.C., and we never had a better. He knows the game, though I believe he never played cricket in his life. But then he knows most things, and has never done any of them. He has never even married, and never opened his lips in the House of Lords. Yet they say there is no better brain in the August assembly, and he certainly made us a wonderful speech last time the Australians were over. He has read everything and (to his credit in these days) never written a line. All. round he is a whale for theory and a sprat for practice—but he looks quite capable of both at crime!"

I now longed to behold this remarkable peer, in the flesh, and with the greater curiosity since another of the things which he evidently never did was to have his photograph published for the benefit of the vulgar. I told Raffles that I would dine with him at Lord Thornaby's, and he nodded as though I had not hesitated for a moment. I see now how deftly he had disposed of my reluctance. No doubt he had thought it all. out before: his little speeches look sufficiently premeditated as I set them down at the dictates of an excellent memory. Let it, however, be borne in mind that Raffles did not talk exactly like a Raffles book: he said the things, but he did not say them in so many consecutive breaths. They were punctuated by puffs from his eternal cigarette, and the punctuation was often in the nature of a line of asterisks, while he took a silent turn up and down his room. Nor was he ever more deliberate than when he seemed most nonchalant and spontaneous. I came to see it in the end. But these were early days, in which he was more plausible to me than I can hope to render him to another human being.

And I saw a good deal of Raffles just then; it was, in fact, the one period at which I can remember his coming round to see me more frequently than I went round to him. Of course he would come at his own odd hours, often just as one was dressing to go out and dine, and I can even remember finding him there when I returned, for I had long since given him a key of the flat. It was the inhospitable month of February, and I can recall more than one cosy evening when we discussed anything and everything but our own malpractices; indeed, there were none to discuss just then. Raffles, on the contrary, was showing himself with some industry in the most respectable society, and by his advice I used the club more than ever.

"There is nothing like it at this time of year," said he. "In the summer I have my cricket to provide me with decent employment in the sight of men. Keep yourself before the public from morning to night, and they'll never think of you in the still small hours."

Our behavior, in fine, had so long been irreproachable that I rose without misgiving on the morning of Lord Thornaby's dinner to the other Criminologists and guests. My chief anxiety was to arrive under the aegis of my brilliant friend, and I had begged him to pick me up on his way; but at five minutes to the appointed hour there was no sign of Raffles or his cab. We were bidden at a quarter to eight for eight o'clock, so after all. I had to hurry off alone.

Fortunately, Thornaby House is almost at the end of my street that was; and it seemed to me another fortunate circumstance that the house stood back, as it did and does, in its own August courtyard; for, as I was about to knock, a hansom came twinkling in behind me, and I drew back, hoping it was Raffles at the last moment. It was not, and I knew it in time to melt from the porch, and wait yet another minute in the shadows, since others were as late as I. And out jumped these others, chattering in stage whispers as they paid their cab.

"Thornaby has a bet about it with Freddy Vereker, who can't come, I hear. Of course, it won t be lost or won to-night. But the dear man thinks he's been invited as a cricketer!"

"I don't believe he's the other thing," said a voice as brusque as the first was bland. "I believe it's all. bunkum. I wish I didn't, but I do!"

"I think you'll find it's more than that," rejoined the other, as the doors opened and swallowed the pair.

I flung out limp hands and smote the air. Raffles bidden to what he had well called this "gruesome board," not as a cricketer but, clearly, as a suspected criminal! Raffles wrong all. the time, and I right for once in my original apprehension! And still no Raffles in sight—no Raffles to warn—no Raffles, and the clocks striking eight!

Well may I shirk the psychology of such a moment, for my belief is that the striking clocks struck out all. power of thought and feeling, and that I played my poor part the better for that blessed surcease of intellectual sensation. On the other hand, I was never more alive to the purely objective impressions of any hour of my existence, and of them the memory is startling to this day. I hear my mad knock at the double doors; they fly open in the middle, and it is like some sumptuous and solemn rite. A long slice of silken-legged lackey is seen on either hand; a very prelate of a butler bows a benediction from the sanctuary steps. I breathe more freely when I reach a book-lined library where a mere handful of men do not overflow the Persian rug before the fire. One of them is Raffles, who is talking to a large man with the brow of a demi-god and the eyes and jowl of a degenerate bulldog. And this is our noble host.

Lord Thornaby stared at me with inscrutable stolidity as we shook hands, and at once handed me over to a tall, ungainly man whom he addressed as Ernest, but whose surname I never learned. Ernest in turn introduced me, with a shy and clumsy courtesy, to the two remaining guests. They were the pair who had driven up in the hansom; one turned out to be Kingsmill, Q.C.; the other I knew at a glance from his photographs as Parrington, the backwoods novelist. They were admirable foils to each other, the barrister being plump and dapper, with a Napoleonic cast of countenance, and the author one of the shaggiest dogs I have ever seen in evening-clothes. Neither took much stock of me, but both had an eye on Raffles as I exchanged a few words with each in turn. Dinner, however, was immediately announced, and the six of us had soon taken our places round a brilliant little table stranded in a great dark room.

I had not been prepared for so small a party, and at first I felt relieved. If the worst came to the worst, I was fool enough to say in my heart, they were but two to one. But I was soon sighing for that safety which the adage associates with numbers. We were far too few for the confidential duologue with one's neighbor in which I, at least, would have taken refuge from the perils of a general conversation. And the general conversation soon resolved itself into an attack, so subtly concerted and so artistically delivered that I could not conceive how Raffles should ever know it for an attack, and that against himself, or how to warn him of his peril. But to this day I am not convinced that I also was honored by the suspicions of the club; it may have been so, and they may have ignored me for the bigger game.

It was Lord Thornaby himself who fired the first shot, over the very sherry. He had Raffles on his right hand, and the backwoodsman of letters on his left. Raffles was hemmed in by the law on his right, while I sat between Parrington and Ernest, who took the foot of the table, and seemed a sort of feudatory cadet of the noble house. But it was the motley lot of us that my lord addressed, as he sat back blinking his baggy eyes.

"Mr. Raffles," said he, "has been telling me about that poor fellow who suffered the extreme penalty last March. A great end, gentlemen, a great end! It is true that he had been unfortunate enough to strike a jugular vein, but his own end should take its place among the most glorious traditions of the gallows. You tell them Mr. Raffles: it will be as new to my friends as it is to me."

"I tell the tale as I heard it last time I played at Trent Bridge; it was never in the papers, I believe," said Raffles gravely. "You may remember the tremendous excitement over the Test Matches out in Australia at the time: it seems that the result of the crucial game was expected on the condemned man's last day on earth, and he couldn't rest until he knew it. We pulled it off, if you recollect, and he said it would make him swing happy."

"Tell 'em what else he said!" cried Lord Thornaby, rubbing his podgy hands.

"The chaplain remonstrated with him on his excitement over a game at such a time, and the convict is said to have replied: 'Why, it's the first thing they'll ask me at the other end of the drop!'"

The story was new even to me, but I had no time to appreciate its points. My concern was to watch its effect upon the other members of the party. Ernest, on my left, doubled up with laughter, and tittered and shook for several minutes. My other neighbor, more impressionable by temperament, winced first, and then worked himself into a state of enthusiasm which culminated in an assault upon his shirt-cuff with a joiner's pencil. Kingsmill, Q.C., beaming tranquilly on Raffles, seemed the one least impressed, until he spoke.

"I am glad to hear that," he remarked in a high bland voice. "I thought that man would die game."

"Did you know anything about him, then?" inquired Lord Thornaby.

"I led for the Crown," replied the barrister, with a twinkle. "You might almost say that I measured the poor man's neck."

The point must have been quite unpremeditated; it was not the less effective for that. Lord Thornaby looked askance at the callous silk. It was some moments before Ernest tittered and Parrington felt for his pencil; and in the interim I had made short work of my hock, though it was Johannisberger. As for Raffles, one had but to see his horror to feel how completely he was off his guard.

"In itself, I have heard, it was not a sympathetic case?" was the remark with which he broke the general silence.

"Not a bit."

"That must have been a comfort to you," said Raffles dryly.

"It would have been to me," vowed our author, while the barrister merely smiled. "I should have been very sorry to have had a hand in hanging Peckham and Solomons the other day."

"Why Peckham and Solomons?" inquired my lord.

"They never meant to kill that old lady."

"But they strangled her in her bed with her own pillow-case!"

"I don't care," said the uncouth scribe. "They didn't break in for that. They never thought of scragging her. The foolish old person would make a noise, and one of them tied too tight. I call it jolly bad luck on them."

"On quiet, harmless, well-behaved thieves," added Lord Thornaby, "in the unobtrusive exercise of their humble avocation."

And, as he turned to Raffles with his puffy smile, I knew that we had reached that part of the programme which had undergone rehearsal: it had been perfectly timed to arrive with the champagne, and I was not afraid to signify my appreciation of that small mercy. But Raffles laughed so quickly at his lordship's humor, and yet with such a natural restraint, as to leave no doubt that he had taken kindly to my own old part, and was playing the innocent inimitably in his turn, by reason of his very innocence. It was a poetic judgment on old Raffles, and in my momentary enjoyment of the novel situation I was able to enjoy some of the good things of this rich man's table. The saddle of mutton more than justified its place in the menu; but it had not spoiled me for my wing of pheasant, and I was even looking forward to a sweet, when a further remark from the literary light recalled me from the table to its talk.

"But, I suppose," said he to Kingsmill, "it's many a burglar you've restored to his friends and his relations'?"

"Let us say many a poor fellow who has been charged with burglary," replied the cheery Q.C. "It's not quite the same thing, you know, nor is 'many' the most accurate word. I never touch criminal work in town."

"It's the only kind I should care about," said the novelist, eating jelly with a spoon.

"I quite agree with you," our host chimed in. "And of all. the criminals one might be called upon to defend, give me the enterprising burglar."

"It must be the breeziest branch of the business," remarked Raffles, while I held my breath.

But his touch was as light as gossamer, and his artless manner a triumph of even his incomparable art. Raffles was alive to the danger at last. I saw him refuse more champagne, even as I drained my glass again. But it was not the same danger to us both. Raffles had no reason to feel surprise or alarm at such a turn in a conversation frankly devoted to criminology; it must have been as inevitable to him as it was sinister to me, with my fortuitous knowledge of the suspicions that were entertained. And there was little to put him on his guard in the touch of his adversaries, which was only less light than his own.

"I am not very fond of Mr. Sikes," announced the barrister, like a man who had got his cue.

"But he was prehistoric," rejoined my lord. "A lot of blood has flowed under the razor since the days of Sweet William."

"True; we have had Peace," said Parrington, and launched out into such glowing details of that criminal's last moments that I began to hope the diversion might prove permanent. But Lord Thornaby was not to be denied.

"William and Charles are both dead monarchs," said he. "The reigning king in their department is the fellow who gutted poor Danby's place in Bond Street."

There was a guilty silence on the part of the three conspirators—for I had long since persuaded myself that Ernest was not in their secret—and then my blood froze.

"I know him well," said Raffles, looking up.

Lord Thornaby stared at him in consternation. The smile on the Napoleonic countenance of the barrister looked forced and frozen for the first time during the evening. Our author, who was nibbling cheese from a knife, left a bead of blood upon his beard. The futile Ernest alone met the occasion with a hearty titter.

"What!" cried my lord. "You know the thief?"

"I wish I did," rejoined Raffles, chuckling. "No, Lord Thornaby, I only meant the jeweller, Danby. I go to him when I want a wedding present."

I heard three deep breaths drawn as one before I drew my own.

"Rather a coincidence," observed our host dryly, "for I believe you also know the Milchester people, where Lady Melrose had her necklace stolen a few months afterward."

"I was staying there at the time," said Raffles eagerly. No snob was ever quicker to boast of basking in the smile of the great.

"We believe it to be the same man," said Lord Thornaby, speaking apparently for the Criminologists' Club, and with much less severity of voice.

"I only wish I could come across him," continued Raffles heartily. "He's a criminal much more to my mind than your murderers who swear on the drop or talk cricket in the condemned cell!"

"He might be in the house now," said Lord Thornaby, looking Raffles in the face. But his manner was that of an actor in an unconvincing part and a mood to play it gamely to the bitter end; and he seemed embittered, as even a rich man may be in the moment of losing a bet.

"What a joke if he were!" cried the Wild West writer.

"Absit omen!" murmured Raffles, in better taste.

"Still, I think you'll find it's a favorite time," argued Kingsmill, Q.C. "And it would be quite in keeping with the character of this man, so far as it is known, to pay a little visit to the president of the Criminologists' Club, and to choose the evening on which he happens to be entertaining the other members."

There was more conviction in this sally than in that of our noble host; but this I attributed to the trained and skilled dissimulation of the bar. Lord Thornaby, however, was not to be amused by the elaboration of his own idea, and it was with some asperity that he called upon the butler, now solemnly superintending the removal of the cloth.

"Leggett! Just send up-stairs to see if all. the doors are open and the rooms in proper order. That's an awful idea of yours, Kingsmill, or of mine!" added my lord, recovering the courtesy of his order by an effort that I could follow. "We should look fools. I don't know which of us it was, by the way, who seduced the rest from the main stream of blood into this burglarious backwater. Are you familiar with De Quincey's masterpiece on 'Murder as a Fine Art,' Mr. Raffles?"

"I believe I once read it," replied Raffles doubtfully.

"You must read it again," pursued the earl. "It is the last word on a great subject; all. we can hope to add is some baleful illustration or bloodstained footnote, not unworthy of De Quincey's text. "Well, Leggett?"

The venerable butler stood wheezing at his elbow. I had not hitherto observed that the man was an asthmatic.

"I beg your lordship's pardon, but I think your lordship must have forgotten."

The voice came in rude gasps, but words of reproach could scarcely have achieved a finer delicacy.

"Forgotten, Leggett! Forgotten what, may I ask?"

"Locking your lordship's dressing-room door behind your lordship, my lord," stuttered the unfortunate Leggett, in the short spurts of a winded man, a few stertorous syllables at a time. "Been up myself, my lord. Bedroom door—dressing-room door—both locked inside!"

But by this time the noble master was in worse case than the man. His fine forehead was a tangle of livid cords; his baggy jowl filled out like a balloon. In another second he had abandoned his place as our host and fled the room; and in yet another we had forgotten ours as his guests and rushed headlong at his heels.

Raffles was as excited as any of us now: he outstripped us all. The cherubic little lawyer and I had a fine race for the last place but one, which I secured, while the panting butler and his satellites brought up a respectful rear. It was our unconventional author, however, who was the first to volunteer his assistance and advice.

"No use pushing, Thornaby!" cried he. "If it's been done with a wedge and gimlet, you may smash the door, but you'll never force it. Is there a ladder in the place?"

"There's a rope-ladder somewhere, in case of fire, I believe," said my lord vaguely, as he rolled a critical eye over our faces. "Where is it kept, Leggett?"

"William will fetch it, my lord."

And a pair of noble calves went flashing to the upper regions.

"What's the good of bringing it down," cried Parrington, who had thrown back to the wilds in his excitement. "Let him hang it out of the window above your own, and let me climb down and do the rest! I'll undertake to have one or other of these doors open in two twos!"

The fastened doors were at right angles on the landing which we filled between us. Lord Thornaby smiled grimly on the rest of us, when he had nodded and dismissed the author like a hound from the leash.

"It's a good thing we know something about our friend Parrington," said my lord. "He takes more kindly to all. this than I do, I can tell you."

"It's grist to his mill," said Raffles charitably.

"Exactly! We shall have the whole thing in his next book."

"I hope to have it at the Old Bailey first," remarked Kingsmill, Q.C.

"Refreshing to find a man of letters such a man of action too!"

It was Raffles who said this, and the remark seemed rather trite for him, but in the tone there was a something that just caught my private ear. And for once I understood: the officious attitude of Parrington, without being seriously suspicious in itself, was admirably calculated to put a previously suspected person in a grateful shade. This literary adventurer had elbowed Raffles out of the limelight, and gratitude for the service was what I had detected in Raffles's voice. No need to say how grateful I felt myself. But my gratitude was shot with flashes of unwonted insight. Parrington was one of those who suspected Raffles, or, at all. events, one who was in the secret of those suspicions. What if he had traded on the suspect's presence in the house? What if he were a deep villain himself, and the villain of this particular piece? I had made up my mind about him, and that in a tithe of the time I take to make it up as a rule, when we heard my man in the dressing-room. He greeted us with an impudent shout; in a few moments the door was open, and there stood Parrington, flushed and dishevelled, with a gimlet in one hand and a wedge in the other.

Within was a scene of eloquent disorder. Drawers had been pulled out, and now stood on end, their contents heaped upon the carpet. Wardrobe doors stood open; empty stud-cases strewed the floor; a clock, tied up in a towel, had been tossed into a chair at the last moment. But a long tin lid protruded from an open cupboard in one corner. And one had only to see Lord Thornaby's wry face behind the lid to guess that it was bent over a somewhat empty tin trunk.

"What a rum lot to steal!" said he, with a twitch of humor at the corners of his canine mouth. "My peer's robes, with coronet complete!"

We rallied round him in a seemly silence. I thought our scribe would put in his word. But even he either feigned or felt a proper awe.

"You may say it was a rum place to keep 'em," continued Lord Thornaby. "But where would you gentlemen stable your white elephants? And these were elephants as white as snow; by Jove, I'll job them for the future!"

And he made merrier over his loss than any of us could have imagined the minute before; but the reason dawned on me a little later, when we all. trooped down-stairs, leaving the police in possession of the theatre of crime. Lord Thornaby linked arms with Raffles as he led the way. His step was lighter, his gayety no longer sardonic; his very looks had improved. And I divined the load that had been lifted from the hospitable heart of our host.

"I only wish," said he, "that this brought us any nearer to the identity of the gentleman we were discussing at dinner, for, of course, we owe it to all. our instincts to assume that it was he."

"I wonder!" said old Raffles, with a foolhardy glance at me.

"But I'm sure of it, my dear sir," cried my lord. "The audacity is his and his alone. I look no further than the fact of his honoring me on the one night of the year when I endeavor to entertain my brother Criminologists. That's no coincidence, sir, but a deliberate irony, which would have occurred to no other criminal mind in England."

"You may be right," Raffles had the sense to say this time, though I flattered myself it was my face that made him.

"What is still more certain," resumed our host, "is that no other criminal in the world would have crowned so delicious a conception with so perfect an achievement. I feel sure the inspector will agree with us."

The policeman in command had knocked and been admitted to the library as Lord Thornaby spoke.

"I didn't hear what you said, my lord."

"Merely that the perpetrator of this amusing outrage can be no other than the swell mobsman who relieved Lady Melrose of her necklace and poor Danby of half his stock a year or two ago."

"I believe your lordship has hit the nail on the head."

"The man who took the Thimblely diamonds and returned them to Lord Thimblely, you know."

"Perhaps he'll treat your lordship the same."

"Not he! I don't mean to cry over my spilt milk. I only wish the fellow joy of all. he had time to take. Anything fresh up-stain by the way?"

"Yes, my lord: the robbery took place between a quarter past eight and the half-hour."

"How on earth do you know?"

"The clock that was tied up in the towel had stopped at twenty past."

"Have you interviewed my man?"

"I have, my lord. He was in your lordship's room until close on the quarter, and all. was as it should be when he left it."

"Then do you suppose the burglar was in hiding in the house?"

"It's impossible to say, my lord. He's not in the house now, for he could only be in your lordship's bedroom or dressing-room, and we have searched every inch of both."

Lord Thornaby turned to us when the inspector had retreated, caressing his peaked cap.

"I told him to clear up these points first," he explained, jerking his head toward the door. "I had reason to think my man had been neglecting his duties up there. I am glad to find myself mistaken."

I ought to have been no less glad to see my own mistake. My suspicions of our officious author were thus proved to have been as wild as himself. I owed the man no grudge, and yet in my human heart I felt vaguely disappointed. My theory had gained color from his behavior ever since he had admitted us to the dressing-room; it had changed all. at once from the familiar to the morose; and only now was I just enough to remember that Lord Thornaby, having tolerated those familiarities as long as they were connected with useful service, had administered a relentless snub the moment that service had been well and truly performed.

But if Parrington was exonerated in my mind, so also was Raffles reinstated in the regard of those who had entertained a far graver and more dangerous hypothesis. It was a miracle of good luck, a coincidence among coincidences, which had white-washed him in their sight at the very moment when they were straining the expert eye to sift him through and through. But the miracle had been performed, and its effect was visible in every face and audible in every voice. I except Ernest, who could never have been in the secret; moreover, that gay Criminologist had been palpably shaken by his first little experience of crime. But the other three vied among themselves to do honor where they had done injustice. I heard Kingsmill, Q.C., telling Raffles the best time to catch him at chambers, and promising a seat in court for any trial he might ever like to hear. Parrington spoke of a presentation set of his books, and in doing homage to Raffles made his peace with our host. As for Lord Thornaby, I did overhear the name of the Athenaeum Club, a reference to his friends on the committee, and a whisper (as I thought) of Rule II.

The police were still in possession when we went our several ways, and it was all. that I could do to drag Raffles up to my rooms, though, as I have said, they were just round the corner. He consented at last as a lesser evil than talking of the burglary in the street; and in my rooms I told him of his late danger and my own dilemma, of the few words I had overheard in the beginning, of the thin ice on which he had cut fancy figures without a crack. It was all. very well for him. He had never realized his peril. But let him think of me—listening, watching, yet unable to lift a finger—unable to say one warning word.

Raffles suffered me to finish, but a weary sigh followed the last symmetrical whiff of a Sullivan which he flung into my fire before he spoke.

"No, I won't have another, thank you. I'm going to talk to you, Bunny. Do you really suppose I didn't see through these wiseacres from the first?"

I flatly refused to believe he had done so before that evening. Why had he never mentioned his idea to me? It had been quite the other way, as I indignantly reminded Raffles. Did he mean me to believe he was the man to thrust his head into the lion's mouth for fun? And what point would there be in dragging me there to see the fun?

"I might have wanted you, Bunny. I very nearly did."

"For my face?"

"It has been my fortune before to-night, Bunny. It has also given me more confidence than you are likely to believe at this time of day. You stimulate me more than you think."

"Your gallery and your prompter's box in one?"

"Capital, Bunny! But it was no joking matter with me either, my dear fellow; it was touch-and-go at the time. I might have called on you at any moment, and it was something to know I should not have called in vain."

"But what to do, Raffles?"

"Fight our way out and bolt!" he answered, with a mouth that meant it, and a fine gay glitter of the eyes.

I shot out of my chair.

"You don't mean to tell me you had a hand in the job?"

"I had the only hand in it, my dear Bunny."

"Nonsense! You were sitting at table at the time. No, but you may have taken some other fellow into the show. I always thought you would!"

"One's quite enough, Bunny," said Raffles dryly; he leaned back in his chair and took out another cigarette. And I accepted of yet another from his case; for it was no use losing one's temper with Raffles; and his incredible statement was not, after all., to be ignored.

"Of course," I went on, "if you really had brought off this thing on your own, I should be the last to criticise your means of reaching such an end. You have not only scored off a far superior force, which had laid itself out to score off you, but you have put them in the wrong about you, and they'll eat out of your hand for the rest of their days. But don't ask me to believe that you've done all. this alone! By George," I cried, in a sudden wave of enthusiasm, "I don't care how you've done it or who has helped you. It's the biggest thing you ever did in your life!"

And certainly I had never seen Raffles look more radiant, or better pleased with the world and himself, or nearer that elation which he usually left to me.

"Then you shall hear all. about it, Bunny, if you'll do what I ask you."

"Ask away, old chap, and the thing's done."

"Switch off the electric lights."

"All. of them?"

"I think so."

"There, then."

"Now go to the back window and up with the blind."

"Well?"?"

"I'm coming to you. Splendid! I never had a look so late as this. It's the only window left alight in the house!"

His cheek against the pane, he was pointing slightly downward and very much aslant through a long lane of mews to a little square light like a yellow tile at the end. But I had opened the window and leaned out before I saw it for myself.

"You don't mean to say that's Thornaby House?"

I was not familiar with the view from my back windows.

"Of course I do, you rabbit! Have a look through your own race-glass. It has been the most useful thing of all."

But before I had the glass in focus more scales had fallen from my eyes; and now I knew why I had seen so much of Raffles these last few weeks, and why he had always come between seven and eight o'clock in the evening, and waited at this very window, with these very glasses at his eyes. I saw through them sharply now. The one lighted window pointed out by Raffles came tumbling into the dark circle of my vision. I could not see into the actual room, but the shadows of those within were quite distinct on the lowered blind. I even thought a black thread still dangled against the square of light. It was, it must be, the window to which the intrepid Parrington had descended from the one above.

"Exactly!" said Raffles in answer to my exclamation. "And that's the window I have been watching these last few weeks. By daylight you can see the whole lot above the ground floor on this side of the house; and by good luck one of them is the room in which the master of the house arrays himself in all. his nightly glory. It was easily spotted by watching at the right time. I saw him shaved one morning before you were up! In the evening his valet stays behind to put things straight; and that has been the very mischief. In the end I had to find out something about the man, and wire to him from his girl to meet her outside at eight o'clock. Of course he pretends he was at his post at the time: that I foresaw, and did the poor fellow's work before my own. I folded and put away every garment before I permitted myself to rag the room."

"I wonder you had time!"

"It took me one more minute, and it put the clock on exactly fifteen. By the way, I did that literally, of course, in the case of the clock they found. It's an old dodge, to stop a clock and alter the time; but you must admit that it looked as though one had wrapped it up all. ready to cart away. There was thus any amount of prima-fade evidence of the robbery having taken place when we were all. at table. As a matter of fact, Lord Thornaby left his dressing-room one minute, his valet followed him the minute after, and I entered the minute after that."

"Through the window?"

"To be sure. I was waiting below in the garden. You have to pay for your garden in town, in more ways than one. You know the wall, of course, and that jolly old postern? The lock was beneath contempt."

"But what about the window? It's on the first floor, isn't it?"

Raffles took up the cane which he had laid down with his overcoat. It was a stout bamboo with a polished ferule. He unscrewed the ferule, and shook out of the cane a diminishing series of smaller canes, exactly like a child's fishing-rod, which I afterward found to have been their former state. A double hook of steel was now produced and quickly attached to the tip of the top joint; then Raffles undid three buttons of his waistcoat; and lapped round and round his waist was the finest of Manila ropes, with the neatest of foot-loops at regular intervals.

"Is it necessary to go any further?" asked Raffles when he had unwound the rope. "This end is made fast to that end of the hook, the other half of the hook fits over anything that comes its way, and you leave your rod dangling while you swarm up your line. Of course, you must know what you've got to hook on to; but a man who has had a porcelain bath fixed in his dressing-room is the man for me. The pipes were all. outside, and fixed to the wall in just the right place. You see I had made a reconnaissance by day in addition to many by night; it would hardly have been worth while constructing my ladder on chance."

"So you made it on purpose!"

"My dear Bunny," said Raffles, as he wound the hemp girdle round his waist once more, "I never did care for ladder work, but I always said that if I ever used a ladder it should be the best of its kind yet invented. This one may come in useful again."

"But how long did the whole thing take you?"

"From mother earth, to mother earth? About five minutes, to-night, and one of those was spent in doing another man's work."

"What!" I cried. "You mean to tell me you climbed up and down, in and out, and broke into that cupboard and that big tin box, and wedged up the doors and cleared out with a peer's robes and all. the rest of it in five minutes?"

"Of course I don't, and of course I didn't."

"Then what do you mean, and what did you do?"

"Made two bites at the cherry, Bunny! I had a dress rehearsal in the dead of last night, and it was then I took the swag. Our noble friend was snoring next door all. the time, but the effort may still stand high among my small exploits, for I not only took all. I wanted, but left the whole place exactly as I found it, and shut things after me like a good little boy. All. that took a good deal longer; to-night I had simply to rag the room a bit, sweep up some studs and links, and leave ample evidence of having boned those rotten robes to-night. That, if you come to think of it, was what you writing chaps would call the quintessential Q.E.F. I have not only shown these dear Criminologists that I couldn't possibly have done this trick, but that there's some other fellow who could and did, and whom they've been perfect asses to confuse with me."

You may figure me as gazing on Raffles all. this time in mute and rapt amazement. But I had long been past that pitch. If he had told me now that he had broken into the Bank of England, or the Tower, I should not have disbelieved him for a moment. I was prepared to go home with him to the Albany and find the regalia under his bed. And I took down my overcoat as he put on his. But Raffles would not hear of my accompanying him that night.

"No, my dear Bunny, I am short of sleep and fed up with excitement. You mayn't believe it—you may look upon me as a plaster devil—but those five minutes you wot of were rather too crowded even for my taste. The dinner was nominally at a quarter to eight, and I don't mind telling you now that I counted on twice as long as I had. But no one came until twelve minutes to, and so our host took his time. I didn't want to be the last to arrive, and I was in the drawing-room five minutes before the hour. But it was a quicker thing than I care about, when all. is said."

And his last word on the matter, as he nodded and went his way, may well be mine; for one need be no criminologist, much less a member of the Criminologists' Club, to remember what Raffles did with the robes and coronet of the Right Hon. the Earl of Thornaby, K.G. He did with them exactly what he might have been expected to do by the gentlemen with whom he had foregathered; and he did it in a manner so characteristic of himself as surely to remove from their minds the last aura of the idea that he and himself were the same person. Carter Paterson was out of the question, and any labelling or addressing to be avoided on obvious grounds. But Raffles stabled the white elephants in the cloak-room at Charing Cross—and sent Lord Thornaby the ticket.

The Field of Phillipi

Nipper Nasmyth had been head of our school when Raffles was captain of cricket. I believe he owed his nickname entirely to the popular prejudice against a day-boy; and in view of the special reproach which the term carried in my time, as also of the fact that his father was one of the school trustees, partner in a banking firm of four resounding surnames, and manager of the local branch, there can be little doubt that the stigma was undeserved. But we did not think so then, for Nasmyth was unpopular with high and low, and appeared to glory in the fact. A swollen conscience caused him to see and hear even more than was warranted by his position, and his uncompromising nature compelled him to act on whatsoever he heard or saw: a savage custodian of public morals, he had in addition a perverse enthusiasm for lost causes, loved a minority for its own sake, and untenable tenets for theirs. Such, at all. events, was my impression of Nipper Nasmyth, after my first term, which was also his last I had never spoken to him, but I had heard him speak with extraordinary force and fervor in the school debates. I carried a clear picture of his unkempt hair, his unbrushed coat, his dominant spectacles, his dogmatic jaw. And it was I who knew the combination at a glance, after years and years, when the fateful whim seized Raffles to play once more in the Old Boys' Match, and his will took me down with him to participate in the milder festivities of Founder's Day.

It was, however, no ordinary occasion. The bicentenary loomed but a year ahead, and a movement was on foot to mark the epoch with an adequate statue of our pious founder. A special meeting was to be held at the school-house, and Raffles had been specially invited by the new head master, a man of his own standing, who had been in the eleven with him up at Cambridge. Raffles had not been near the old place for years; but I had never gone down since the day I left; and I will not dwell on the emotions which the once familiar journey awakened in my unworthy bosom. Paddington was alive with Old Boys of all. ages—but very few of ours—if not as lively as we used to make it when we all. landed back for the holidays. More of us had moustaches and cigarettes and "loud" ties. That was all. Yet of the throng, though two or three looked twice and thrice at Raffles, neither he nor I knew a soul until we had to change at the junction near our journey's end, when, as I say, it was I who recognized Nipper Nasmyth at sight.

The man was own son of the boy we both remembered. He had grown a ragged beard and a moustache that hung about his face like a neglected creeper. He was stout and bent and older than his years. But he spurned the platform with a stamping stride which even I remembered in an instant, and which was enough for Raffles before he saw the man's face.

"The Nipper it is!" he cried. "I could swear to that walk in a pantomime procession! See the independence in every step: that's his heel on the neck of the oppressor: it's the nonconformist conscience in baggy breeches. I must speak to him, Bunny. There was a lot of good in the old Nipper, though he and I did bar each other."

And in a moment he had accosted the man by the boy's nickname, obviously without thinking of an affront which few would have read in that hearty open face and hand.

"My name's Nasmyth," snapped the other, standing upright to glare.

"Forgive me," said Raffles undeterred. "One remembers a nickname and forgets all. it never used to mean. Shake hands, my dear fellow! I'm Raffles. It must be fifteen years since we met."

"At least," replied Nasmyth coldly; but he could no longer refuse Raffles his hand. "So you are going down," he sneered, "to this great gathering?" And I stood listening at my distance, as though still in the middle fourth.

"Rather!" cried Raffles. "I'm afraid I have let myself lose touch, but I mean to turn over a new leaf. I suppose that isn't necessary in your case, Nasmyth?"

He spoke with an enthusiasm rare indeed in him: it had grown upon Raffles in the train; the spirit of his boyhood had come rushing back at fifty miles an hour. He might have been following some honorable calling in town; he might have snatched this brief respite from a distinguished but exacting career. I am convinced that it was I alone who remembered at that moment the life we were really leading at that time. With me there walked this skeleton through every waking hour that was to follow. I shall endeavor not to refer to it again. Yet it should not be forgotten that my skeleton was always there.

"It certainly is not necessary in my case," replied Nasmyth, still as stiff as any poker. "I happen to be a trustee."

"Of the school?"

"Like my father before me."

"I congratulate you, my dear fellow!" cried the hearty Raffles—a younger Raffles than I had ever known in town.

"I don't know that you need," said Nasmyth sourly.

"But it must be a tremendous interest. And the proof is that you're going down to this show, like all. the rest of us."

"No, I'm not. I live there, you see."

And I think the Nipper recalled that name as he ground his heel upon an unresponsive flagstone.

"But you're going to this meeting at the school-house, surely?"

"I don't know. If I do there may be squalls. I don't know what you think about this precious scheme Raffles, but I . . ."

The ragged beard stuck out, set teeth showed through the wild moustache, and in a sudden outpouring we had his views. They were narrow and intemperate and perverse as any I had heard him advocate as the firebrand of the Debating Society in my first term. But they were stated with all. the old vim and venom. The mind of Nasmyth had not broadened with the years, but neither had its natural force abated, nor that of his character either. He spoke with great vigor at the top of his voice; soon we had a little crowd about us; but the tall collars and the broad smiles of the younger Old Boys did not deter our dowdy demagogue. Why spend money on a man who had been dead two hundred years? What good could it do him or the school? Besides, he was only technically our founder. He had not founded a great public school. He had founded a little country grammar school which had pottered along for a century and a half. The great public school was the growth of the last fifty years, and no credit to the pillar of piety. Besides, he was only nominally pious. Nasmyth had made researches, and he knew. And why throw good money after a bad man?

"Are there many of your opinion?" inquired Raffles, when the agitator paused for breath. And Nasmyth beamed on us with flashing eyes.

"Not one to my knowledge as yet," said he. "But we shall see after to-morrow night. I hear it's to be quite an exceptional gathering this year; let us hope it may contain a few sane men. There are none on the present staff, and I only know of one among the trustees!"

Raffles refrained from smiling as his dancing eye met mine.

"I can understand your view," he said. "I am not sure that I don't share it to some extent. But it seems to me a duty to support a general movement like this even if it doesn't take the direction or the shape of our own dreams. I suppose you yourself will give something, Nasmyth?"

"Give something? I? Not a brass farthing!" cried the implacable banker. "To do so would be to stultify my whole position. I cordially and conscientiously disapprove of the whole thing, and shall use all. my influence against it. No, my good sir, I not only don't subscribe myself, but I hope to be the means of nipping a good many subscriptions in the bud."

I was probably the only one who saw the sudden and yet subtle change in Raffles—the hard mouth, the harder eye. I, at least, might have foreseen the sequel then and there. But his quiet voice betrayed nothing, as he inquired whether Nasmyth was going to speak at next night's meeting. Nasmyth said he might, and certainly warned us what to expect. He was still fulminating when our train came in.

"Then we meet again at Philippi," cried Raffles in gay adieu. "For you have been very frank with us all., Nasmyth, and I'll be frank enough in my turn to tell you that I've every intention of speaking on the other side!"

It happened that Raffles had been asked to speak by his old college friend, the new head master. Yet it was not at the school-house that he and I were to stay, but at the house that we had both been in as boys. It also had changed hands: a wing had been added, and the double tier of tiny studies made brilliant with electric light. But the quad and the fives-courts did not look a day older; the ivy was no thicker round the study windows; and in one boy's castle we found the traditional print of Charing Cross Bridge which had knocked about our studies ever since a son of the contractor first sold it when he left. Nay, more, there was the bald remnant of a stuffed bird which had been my own daily care when it and I belonged to Raffles. And when we all. filed in to prayers, through the green baize door which still separated the master's part of the house from that of the boys, there was a small boy posted in the passage to give the sign of silence to the rest assembled in the hall, quite identically as in the dim old days; the picture was absolutely unchanged; it was only we who were out of it in body and soul.

On our side of the baize door a fine hospitality and a finer flow of spirits were the order of the night. There was a sound representative assortment of quite young Old Boys, to whom ours was a prehistoric time, and in the trough of their modem chaff and chat we old stagers might well have been left far astern of the fun. Yet it was Raffles who was the life and soul of the party, and that not by meretricious virtue of his cricket. There happened not to be another cricketer among us, and it was on their own subjects that Raffles laughed with the lot in turn and in the lump. I never knew him in quite such form. I will not say he was a boy among them, but he was that rarer being, the man of the world who can enter absolutely into the fun and fervor of the salad age. My cares and my regrets had never been more acute, but Raffles seemed a man without either in his life.

He was not, however, the hero of the Old Boys' Match, and that was expected of him by all. the school. There was a hush when he went in, a groan when he came out. I had no reason to suppose he was not trying; these things happen to the cricketer who plays out of his class; but when the great Raffles went on to bowl, and was hit all. over the field, I was not so sure. It certainly failed to affect his spirits; he was more brilliant than ever at our hospitable board; and after dinner came the meeting at which he and Nasmyth were to speak.

It was a somewhat frigid gathering until Nasmyth rose. We had all. dined with our respective hosts, and then repaired to this business in cold blood. Many were lukewarm about it in their hearts; there was a certain amount of mild prejudice, and a greater amount of animal indifference, to be overcome in the opening speech. It is not for me to say whether this was successfully accomplished. I only know how the temperature of that meeting rose with Nipper Nasmyth.

And I dare say, in all. the circumstances of the case, his really was a rather vulgar speech. But it was certainly impassioned, and probably as purely instinctive as his denunciation of all. the causes which appeal to the gullible many without imposing upon the cantankerous few. His arguments, it is true, were merely an elaboration of those with which he had favored some of us already; but they were pointed by a concise exposition of the several definite principles they represented, and barbed with a caustic rhetoric quite admirable in itself. In a word, the manner was worthy of the very foundation it sought to shake, or we had never swallowed such matter without a murmur. As it was, there was a demonstration in the wilderness when the voice ceased crying. But we sat in the deeper silence when Raffles rose to reply.

I leaned forward not to lose a word. I knew my Raffles so well that I felt almost capable of reporting his speech before I heard it. Never was I more mistaken, even in him! So far from a gibe for a gibe and a taunt for a taunt, there never was softer answer than that which A. J. Raffles returned to Nipper Nasmyth before the staring eyes and startled ears of all. assembled. He courteously but firmly refused to believe a word his old friend Nasmyth had said—about himself. He had known Nasmyth for twenty years, and never had he met a dog who barked so loud and bit so little. The fact was that he had far too kind a heart to bite at all. Nasmyth might get up and protest as loud as he liked: the speaker declared he knew him better than Nasmyth knew himself. He had the necessary defects of his great qualities. He was only too good a sportsman. He had a perfect passion for the weaker side. That alone led Nasmyth into such excesses of language as we had all. heard from his lips that night. As for Raffles, he concluded his far too genial remarks by predicting that, whatever Nasmyth might say or think of the new fund, he would subscribe to it as handsomely as any of us, like "the generous good chap" that we all. knew him to be.

Even so did Raffles disappoint the Old Boys in the evening as he had disappointed the school by day. We had looked to him for a noble raillery, a lofty and loyal disdain, and he had fobbed us off with friendly personalities not even in impeccable taste. Nevertheless, this light treatment of a grave offence went far to restore the natural amenities of the occasion. It was impossible even for Nasmyth to reply to it as he might to a more earnest onslaught. He could but smile sardonically, and audibly undertake to prove Raffles a false prophet; and though subsequent speakers were less merciful the note was struck, and there was no more bad blood in the debate. There was plenty, however, in the veins of Nasmyth, as I was to discover for myself before the night was out.

You might think that in the circumstances he would not have attended the head master's ball with which the evening ended; but that would be sadly to misjudge so perverse a creature as the notorious Nipper. He was probably one of those who protest that there is "nothing personal" in their most personal attacks. Not that Nasmyth took this tone about Raffles when he and I found ourselves cheek by jowl against the ballroom wall; he could forgive his franker critics, but not the friendly enemy who had treated him so much more gently than he deserved.

"I seem to have seen you with this great man Raffles," began Nasmyth, as he overhauled me with his fighting eye. "Do you know him well?"

"Intimately."

"I remember now. You were with him when he forced himself upon me on the way down yesterday. He had to tell me who he was. Yet he talks as though we were old friends."

"You were in the upper sixth together," I rejoined, nettled by his tone.

"What does that matter? I am glad to say I had too much self-respect, and too little respect for Raffles, ever to be a friend of his then. I knew too many of the things he did," said Nipper Nasmyth.

His fluent insults had taken my breath. But in a lucky flash I saw my retort.

"You must have had special opportunities of observation, living in the town," said I; and drew first blood between the long hair and the ragged beard; but that was all.

"So he really did get out at nights?" remarked my adversary. "You certainly give your friend away. What's he doing now?"

I let my eyes follow Raffles round the room before replying. He was waltzing with a master's wife—waltzing as he did everything else. Other couples seemed to melt before them. And the woman on his arm looked a radiant girl.

"I meant in town, or wherever he lives his mysterious life," explained Nasmyth, when I told him that he could see for himself. But his clever tone did not trouble me; it was his epithet that caused me to prick my ears. And I found some difficulty in following Raffles right round the room.

"I thought everybody knew what he was doing; he's playing cricket most of his time," was my measured reply; and if it bore an extra touch of insolence, I can honestly ascribe that to my nerves.

"And is that all. he does for a living?" pursued my inquisitor keenly.

"You had better ask Raffles himself," said I to that. "It's a pity you didn't ask him in public, at the meeting!"

But I was beginning to show temper in my embarrassment, and of course that made Nasmyth the more imperturbable.

"Really, he might be following some disgraceful calling, by the mystery you make of it!" he exclaimed. "And for that matter I call first-class cricket a disgraceful calling, when it's followed by men who ought to be gentlemen, but are really professionals in gentlemanly clothing. The present craze for gladiatorial athleticism I regard as one of the great evils of the age; but the thinly veiled professionalism of the so-called amateur is the greatest evil of that craze. Men play for the gentlemen and are paid more than the players who walk out of another gate. In my time there was none of that. Amateurs were amateurs and sport was sport; there were no Raffleses in first-class cricket then. I had forgotten Raffles was a modern first-class cricketer: that explains him. Rather than see my son such another, do you know what I'd prefer to see him?"

I neither knew nor cared: yet a wretched premonitory fascination held me breathless till I was told!.

"I'd prefer to see him a thief!" said Nasmyth savagely; and when his eyes were done with me, he turned upon his heel. So that ended that stage of my discomfiture.

It was only to give place to a worse. Was all. this accident or fell design? Conscience had made a coward of me, and yet what reason had I to disbelieve the worst? We were pirouetting on the edge of an abyss; sooner or later the false step must come and the pit swallow us. I began to wish myself back in London, and I did get back to my room in our old house. My dancing days were already over; there I had taken the one resolution to which I remained as true as better men to better vows; there the painful association was no mere sense of personal unworthiness. I fell to thinking in my room of other dances…and was still smoking the cigarette which Raffles had taught me to appreciate when I looked up to find him regarding me from the door. He had opened it as noiselessly as only Raffles could open doors, and now he closed it in the same professional fashion.

"I missed Achilles hours ago," said he. "And still he's sulking in his tent!"

"I have been," I answered, laughing as he could always make me, "but I'll chuck it if you'll stop and smoke. Our host doesn't mind; there's an ash-tray provided for the purpose. I ought to be sulking between the sheets, but I'm ready to sit up with you till morning."

"We might do worse; but, on the other hand, we might do still better," rejoined Raffles, and for once he resisted the seductive Sullivan. "As a matter of fact, it's morning now; in another hour it will be dawn; and where could day dawn better than in Warfield Woods, or along the Stockley road, or even on the Upper or the Middle? I don't want to turn in, any more than you do. I may as well confess that the whole show down here has exalted me more than anything for years. But if we can't sleep, Bunny, let's have some fresh air instead."

"Has everybody gone to bed?" I asked.

"Long ago. I was the last in. Why?"

"Only it might sound a little odd, our turning out again, if they were to hear us."

Raffles stood over me with a smile made of mischief and cunning; but it was the purest mischief imaginable, the most innocent and comic cunning.

"They shan't hear us at all., Bunny," said he. "I mean to get out as I did in the good old nights. I've been spoiling for the chance ever since I came down. There's not the smallest harm in it now; and if you'll come with me I'll show you how it used to be done."

"But I know," said I. "Who used to haul up the rope after you, and let it down again to the minute?"

Raffles looked down on me from lowered lids, over a smile too humorous to offend.

"My dear good Bunny! And do you suppose that even then I had only one way of doing a thing? I've had a spare loophole all. my life, and when you're ready I'll show you what it was when I was here. Take off those boots, and carry your tennis-shoes; slip on another coat; put out your light; and I'll meet you on the landing in two minutes."

He met me with uplifted finger, and not a syllable; and down-stairs he led me, stocking soles close against the skirting, two feet to each particular step. It must have seemed child's play to Raffles; the old precautions were obviously assumed for my entertainment; but I confess that to me it was all. refreshingly exciting—for once without a risk of durance if we came to grief! With scarcely a creak we reached the hall, and could have walked out of the street door without danger or difficulty. But that would not do for Raffles. He must needs lead me into the boys' part, through the green baize door. It took a deal of opening and shutting, but Raffles seemed to enjoy nothing better than these mock obstacles, and in a few minutes we were resting with sharp ears in the boys' hall.

"Through these windows?" I whispered, when the clock over the piano had had matters its own way long enough to make our minds quite easy.

"How else?" whispered Raffles, as he opened the one on whose ledge our letters used to await us of a morning.

"And then through the quad—"

"And over the gates at the end. No talking, Bunny; there's a dormitory just overhead; but ours was in front, you remember, and if they had ever seen me I should have nipped back this way while they were watching the other."

His finger was on his lips as we got out softly into the starlight. I remember how the gravel hurt as we left the smooth flagged margin of the house for the open quad; but the nearer of two long green seats (whereon you prepared your construe for the second-school in the summer term) was mercifully handy; and once in our rubber soles we had no difficulty in scaling the gates beyond the fives-courts. Moreover, we dropped into a very desert of a country road, nor saw a soul when we doubled back beneath the outer study windows, nor heard a footfall in the main street of the slumbering town. Our own fell like the night-dews and the petals of the poet; but Raffles ran his arm through mine, and would chatter in whispers as we went.

"So you and Nipper had a word—or was it words? I saw you out of the tail of my eye when I was dancing, and I heard you out of the tail of my ear. It sounded like words, Bunny, and I thought I caught my name. He's the most consistent man I know, and the least altered from a boy. But he'll subscribe all. right, you'll see, and be very glad I made him."

I whispered back that I did not believe it for a moment. Raffles had not heard all. Nasmyth had said of him. And neither would he listen to the little I meant to repeat to him; he would but reiterate a conviction so chimerical to my mind that I interrupted in my turn to ask him what ground he had for it.

"I've told you already," said Raffles. "I mean to make him."

"But how?" I asked. "And when, and where?"

"At Philippi, Bunny, where I said I'd see him. What a rabbit you are at a quotation!

"'And I think that the field of Philippi
    Was where Caesar came to an end;
But who gave old Brutus the tip, I
Can't comprehend!'

"You may have forgotten your Shakespeare, Bunny, but you ought to remember that."

And I did, vaguely, but had no idea what it or Raffles meant, as I plainly told him.

"The theatre of war," he answered—"and here we are at the stage door!"

Raffles had stopped suddenly in his walk. It was the last dark hour of the summer night, but the light from a neighboring lamppost showed me the look on his face as he turned.

"I think you also inquired when," he continued. "Well, then, this minute—if you will give me a leg up!"

And behind him, scarcely higher than his head, and not even barred, was a wide window with a wire blind, and the name of Nasmyth among others lettered in gold upon the wire.

"You're never going to break in?"

"This instant, if you'll, help me; in five or ten minutes, if you won't."

"Surely you didn't bring the—the tools?"

He jingled them gently in his pocket.

"Not the whole outfit, Bunny. But you never know when you mayn't want one or two. I'm only thankful I didn't leave the lot behind this time. I very nearly did."

"I must say I thought you would, coming down here," I said reproachfully.

"But you ought to be glad I didn't," he rejoined with a smile. "It's going to mean old Nasmyth's subscription to the Founder's Fund, and that's to be a big one, I promise you! The lucky thing is that I went so far as to bring my bunch of safekeys. Now, are you going to help me use them, or are you not? If so, now's your minute; if not, clear out and be—"

"Not so fast, Raffles," said I testily. "You must have planned this before you came down, or you would never have brought all. those things with you."

"My dear Bunny, they're a part of my kit! I take them wherever I take my evening-clothes. As to this potty bank, I never even thought of it, much less that it would become a public duty to draw a hundred or so without signing for it. That's all. I shall touch, Bunny—I'm not on the make to-night. There's no risk in it either. If I am caught I shall simply sham champagne and stand the racket; it would be an obvious frolic after what happened at that meeting. And they will catch me, if I stand talking here: you run away back to bed—unless you're quite determined to 'give old Brutus the tip!'

Now we had barely been a minute whispering where we stood, and the whole street was still as silent as the tomb. To me there seemed least danger in discussing the matter quietly on the spot. But even as he gave me my dismissal Raffles turned and caught the sill above him, first with one hand and then with the other. His legs swung like a pendulum as he drew himself up with one arm, then shifted the position of the other hand, and very gradually worked himself waist-high with the sill. But the sill was too narrow for him; that was as far as he could get unaided; and it was as much as I could bear to see of a feat which in itself might have hardened my conscience and softened my heart. But I had identified his doggerel verse at last. I am ashamed to say that it was part of a set of my very own writing in the school magazine of my time. So Raffles knew the stuff better than I did myself, and yet scorned to press his flattery to win me over! He had won me: in a second my rounded shoulders were a pedestal for those dangling feet. And before many more I heard the old metallic snap, followed by the raising of a sash so slowly and gently as to be almost inaudible to me listening just below.

Raffles went through hands first, disappeared for an instant, then leaned out, lowering his hands for me.

"Come on, Bunny! You're safer in than out. Hang on to the sill and let me get you under the arms. Now all. together—quietly does it—and over you come!"

No need to dwell on our proceedings in the bank. I myself had small part in the scene, being posted rather in the wings, at the foot of the stairs leading to the private premises in which the manager had his domestic being. But I made my mind easy about him, for in the silence of my watch I soon detected a nasal note overhead, and it was resonant and aggressive as the man himself. Of Raffles, on the contrary, I heard nothing, for he had shut the door between us, and I was to warn him if a single sound came through. I need scarcely add that no warning was necessary during the twenty minutes we remained in the bank. Raffles afterward assured me that nineteen of them had been spent in filing one key; but one of his latest inventions was a little thick velvet bag in which he carried the keys; and this bag had two elastic mouths, which closed so tightly about either wrist that he could file away, inside, and scarcely hear it himself. As for these keys, they were clever counterfeits of typical patterns by two great safe-making firms. And Raffles had come by them in a manner all. his own, which the criminal world may discover for itself.

When he opened the door and beckoned to me, I knew by his face that he had succeeded to his satisfaction, and by experience better than to question him on the point. Indeed, the first thing was to get out of the bank; for the stars were drowning in a sky of ink and water, and it was a comfort to feel that we could fly straight to our beds. I said so in whispers as Raffles cautiously opened our window and peeped out. In an instant his head was in, and for another I feared the worst.

"What was that, Bunny? No, you don't, my son! There's not a soul in sight that I can see, but you never know, and we may as well lay a scent while we're about it. Ready? Then follow me, and never mind the window."

With that he dropped softly into the street, and I after him, turning to the right instead of the left, and that at a brisk trot instead of the innocent walk which had brought us to the bank. Like mice we scampered past the great schoolroom, with its gable snipping a paler sky than ever, and the shadows melting even in the colonnade underneath. Masters' houses flitted by on the left, lesser landmarks on either side, and presently we were running our heads into the dawn, one under either hedge of the Stockley road.

"Did you see that light in Nab's just now?" cried Raffles as he led.

"No; why?" I panted, nearly spent.

"It was in Nab's dressing—room.

"Yes?"

"I've seen it there before," continued Raffles. "He never was a good sleeper, and his ears reach to the street. I wouldn't like to say how often I was chased by him in the small hours! I believe he knew who it was toward the end, but Nab was not the man to accuse you of what he couldn't prove."

I had no breath for comment. And on sped Raffles like a yacht before the wind, and on I blundered like a wherry at sea, making heavy weather all. the way, and nearer foundering at every stride. Suddenly, to my deep relief, Raffles halted, but only to tell me to stop my pipes while he listened.

"It's all. right, Bunny," he resumed, showing me a glowing face in the dawn. "History's on its own tracks once more, and I'll bet you it's dear old Nab on ours! Come on, Bunny; run to the last gasp, and leave the rest to me."

I was past arguing, and away he went. There was no help for it but to follow as best I could. Yet I had vastly preferred to collapse on the spot, and trust to Raffles's resource, as before very long I must. I had never enjoyed long wind and the hours that we kept in town may well have aggravated the deficiency. Raffles, however, was in first-class training from first-class cricket, and he had no mercy on Nab or me. But the master himself was an old Oxford miler, who could still bear it better than I; nay, as I flagged and stumbled, I heard him pounding steadily behind.

"Come on, come on, or he'll do us!" cried Raffles shrilly over his shoulder; and a gruff sardonic laugh came back over mine. It was pearly morning now, but we had run into a shallow mist that took me by the throat and stabbed me to the lungs. I coughed and coughed, and stumbled in my stride, until down I went, less by accident than to get it over, and so lay headlong in my tracks. And old Nab dealt me a verbal kick as he passed.

"You beast!" he growled, as I have known him growl it in form.

But Raffles himself had abandoned the flight on hearing my downfall, and I was on hands and knees just in time to see the meeting between him and old Nab. And there stood Raffles in the silvery mist, laughing with his whole light heart, leaning back to get the full flavor of his mirth; and, nearer me, sturdy old Nab, dour and grim, with beads of dew on the hoary beard that had been lamp-black in our time.

"So I've caught you at last!" said he. "After more years than I mean to count!"

"Then you're luckier than we are, sir," answered Raffles, "for I fear our man has given us the slip."

"Your man!" echoed Nab. His bushy eyebrows had shot up: it was as much as I could do to keep my own in their place.

"We were indulging in the chase ourselves," explained Raffles, "and one of us has suffered for his zeal, as you can see. It is even possible that we, too, have been chasing a perfectly innocent man."

"Not to say a reformed character," said our pursuer dryly. " suppose you don't mean a member of the school?" he added, pinking his man suddenly as of yore, with all. the old barbed acumen. But Raffles was now his match.

"That would be carrying reformation rather far, sir. No, as I say, I may have been mistaken in the first instance; but I had put out my light and was looking out of the window when I saw a fellow behaving quite suspiciously. He was carrying his boots and creeping along in his socks—which must be why you never heard him, sir. They make less noise than rubber soles even—that is, they must, you know! Well, Bunny had just left me, so I hauled him out and we both crept down to play detective. No sign of the fellow! We had a look in the colonnade—I thought I heard him—and that gave us no end of a hunt for nothing. But just as we were leaving he came padding past under our noses, and that's where we took up the chase. Where he'd been in the meantime I have no idea; very likely he'd done no harm; but it seemed worth while finding out. He had too good a start, though, and poor Bunny had too bad a wind."

"You should have gone on and let me rip," said I, climbing to my feet at last.

"As it is, however, we will all. let the other fellow do so," said old Nab in a genial growl. "And you two had better turn into my house and have something to keep the morning cold out."

You may imagine with what alacrity we complied; and yet I am bound to confess that I had never liked Nab at school. I still remember my term in his form. He had a caustic tongue and fine assortment of damaging epithets, most of which were levelled at my devoted skull during those three months. I now discovered that he also kept a particularly mellow Scotch whiskey, an excellent cigar, and a fund of anecdote of which a mordant wit was the worthy bursar. Enough to add that he kept us laughing in his study until the chapel bells rang him out.

As for Raffles, he appeared to me to feel far more compunction for the fable which he had been compelled to foist upon one of the old masters than for the immeasurably graver offence against society and another Old Boy. This, indeed, did not worry him at all.; and the story was received next day with absolute credulity on all. sides. Nasmyth himself was the first to thank us both for our spirited effort on his behalf; and the incident had the ironic effect of establishing an immediate entente cordiale between Raffles and his very latest victim. I must confess, however, that for my own part I was thoroughly uneasy during the Old Boys' second innings, when Raffles made a selfish score, instead of standing by me to tell his own story in his own way. There was never any knowing with what new detail he was about to embellish it: and I have still to receive full credit for the tact that it required to follow his erratic lead convincingly. Seldom have I been more thankful than when our train started next morning, and the poor, unsuspecting Nasmyth himself waved us a last farewell from the platform.

"Lucky we weren't staying at Nab's," said Raffles, as he lit a Sullivan and opened his Daily Mail at its report of the robbery. "There was one thing Nab would have spotted like the downy old bird he always was and will be."

"What was that?"

"The front door must have been found duly barred and bolted in the morning, and yet we let them assume that we came out that way. Nab would have pounced on the point, and by this time we might have been nabbed ourselves."

It was but a little over a hundred sovereigns that Raffles had taken, and, of course, he had resolutely eschewed any and every form of paper money. He posted his own first contribution of twenty-five pounds to the Founder's Fund immediately on our return to town, before rushing off to more first-class cricket, and I gathered that the rest would follow piecemeal as he deemed it safe. By an odd coincidence, however, a mysterious but magnificent donation of a hundred guineas was almost simultaneously received in notes by the treasurer of the Founder's Fund, from one who simply signed himself "Old Boy." The treasurer happened to be our late host, the new man at our old house, and he wrote to congratulate Raffles on what he was pleased to consider a direct result of the latter's speech. I did not see the letter that Raffles wrote in reply, but in due course I heard the name of the mysterious contributor. He was said to be no other than Nipper Nasmyth himself. I asked Raffles if it was true. He replied that he would ask old Nipper point-blank if he came up as usual to the Varsity match, and if they had the luck to meet. And not only did this happen, but I had the greater luck to be walking round the ground with Raffles when we encountered our shabby friend in front of the pavilion.

"My dear fellow," cried Raffles, "I hear it was you who gave that hundred guineas by stealth to the very movement you denounced. Don't deny it, and don't blush to find it fame. Listen to me. There was a great lot in what you said; but it's the kind of thing we ought all. to back, whether we strictly approve of it in our hearts or not."

"Exactly, Raffles, but the fact is—"

"I know what you're going to say. Don't say it. There's not one in a thousand who would do as you've done, and not one in a million who would do it anonymously."

"But what makes you think I did it, Raffles?"

"Everybody is saying so. You will find it all. over the place when you get back. You will find yourself the most popular man down there, Nasmyth!"

I never saw a nobler embarrassment than that of this awkward, ungainly, cantankerous man: all. his angles seemed to have been smoothed away: there was something quite human in the flushed, undecided, wistful face.

"I never was popular in my life," he said. "I don't want to buy my popularity now. To be perfectly candid with you, Raffles—"

"Don't! I can't stop to hear. They're ringing the bell. But you shouldn't have been angry with me for saying you were a generous good chap, Nasmyth, when you were one all. the time. Good-by, old fellow!"

But Nasmyth detained us a second more. His hesitation was at an end. There was a sudden new light in his face.

"Was I?" he cried. "Then I'll make it two hundred, and damn the odds!"

Raffles was a thoughtful man as we went to our seats. He saw nobody, would acknowledge no remark. Neither did he attend to the cricket for the first half-hour after lunch; instead, he eventually invited me to come for a stroll on the practice ground, where, however, we found two chairs aloof from the fascinating throng.

"I am not often sorry, Bunny, as you know," he began. "But I have been sorry since the interval. I've been sorry for poor old Nipper Nasmyth. Did you see the idea of being popular dawn upon him for the first time in his life?"

"I did; but you had nothing to do with that, my dear man."

Raffles shook his head over me as our eyes met. "I had everything to do with it. I tried to make him tell the meanest lie. I made sure he would, and for that matter he nearly did. Then, at the last moment, he saw how to hedge things with his conscience. And his second hundred will be a real gift."

"You mean under his own name—"

"And with his own free-will. My good Bunny, is it possible you don't know what I did with the hundred we drew from that bank!"

"I knew what you were going to do with it," said I. "I didn't know you had actually got further than the twenty-five you told me you were sending as your own contribution."

Raffles rose abruptly from his chair.

"And you actually thought that came out of his money?"

"Naturally."

"In my name?"

"I thought so."

Raffles stared at me inscrutably for some moments, and for some more at the great white numbers over the grand-stand.

"We may as well have another look at the cricket," said he. "It's difficult to see the board from here, but I believe there's another man out."

A Bad Night

There was to be a certain little wedding in which Raffles and I took a surreptitious interest. The bride-elect was living in some retirement, with a recently widowed mother and an asthmatical brother, in a mellow hermitage on the banks of the Mole. The bridegroom was a prosperous son of the same suburban soil which had nourished both families for generations. The wedding presents were so numerous as to fill several rooms at the pretty retreat upon the Mole, and of an intrinsic value calling for a special transaction with the Burglary Insurance Company in Cheapside. I cannot say how Raffles obtained all. this information. I only know that it proved correct in each particular. I was not indeed deeply interested before the event, since Raffles assured me that it was "a one-man job," and naturally intended to be the one man himself. It was only at the eleventh hour that our positions were inverted by the wholly unexpected selection of Raffles for the English team in the Second Test Match.

In a flash I saw the chance of my criminal career. It was some years since Raffles had served his country in these encounters; he had never thought to be called upon again, and his gratification was only less than his embarrassment. The match was at Old Trafford, on the third Thursday, Friday, and Saturday in July; the other affair had been all. arranged for the Thursday night, the night of the wedding at East Molesey. It was for Raffles to choose between the two excitements, and for once I helped him to make up his mind. I duly pointed out to him that in Surrey, at all. events, I was quite capable of taking his place. Nay, more, I insisted at once on my prescriptive right and on his patriotic obligation in the matter. In the country's name and in my own, I implored him to give it and me a chance; and for once, as I say, my arguments prevailed. Raffles sent his telegram—it was the day before the match. We then rushed down to Esher, and over every inch of the ground by that characteristically circuitous route which he enjoined on me for the next night. And at six in the evening I was receiving the last of my many instructions through a window of the restaurant car.

"Only promise me not to take a revolver," said Raffles in a whisper. "Here are my keys; there's an old life-preserver somewhere in the bureau; take that, if you like—though what you take I rather fear you are the chap to use!"

"Then the rope be round my own neck!" I whispered back. "Whatever else I may do, Raffles, I shan't give you away; and you'll find I do better than you think, and am worth trusting with a little more to do, or I'll know the reason why!"

And I meant to know it, as he was borne out of Euston with raised eyebrows, and I turned grimly on my heel. I saw his fears for me; and nothing could have made me more fearless for myself. Raffles had been wrong about me all. these years; now was my chance to set him right. It was galling to feel that he had no confidence in my coolness or my nerve, when neither had ever failed him at a pinch. I had been loyal to him through rough and smooth. In many an ugly corner I had stood as firm as Raffles himself. I was his right hand, and yet he never hesitated to make me his catspaw. This time, at all. events, I should be neither one nor the other; this time I was the understudy playing lead at last; and I wish I could think that Raffles ever realized with what gusto I threw myself into his part.

Thus I was first out of a crowded theatre train at Esher next night, and first down the stairs into the open air. The night was close and cloudy; and the road to Hampton Court, even now that the suburban builder has marked much of it for his own, is one of the darkest I know. The first mile is still a narrow avenue, a mere tunnel of leaves at midsummer; but at that time there was not a lighted pane or cranny by the way. Naturally, it was in this blind reach that I fancied I was being followed. I stopped in my stride; so did the steps I made sure I had heard not far behind; and when I went on, they followed suit. I dried my forehead as I walked, but soon brought myself to repeat the experiment when an exact repetition of the result went to convince me that it had been my own echo all. the time. And since I lost it on getting quit of the avenue, and coming out upon the straight and open road, I was not long in recovering from my scare. But now I could see my way, and found the rest of it without mishap, though not without another semblance of adventure. Over the bridge across the Mole, when about to turn to the left, I marched straight upon a policeman in rubber soles. I had to call him "officer" as I passed, and to pass my turning by a couple of hundred yards, before venturing back another way.

At last I had crept through a garden gate, and round by black windows to a black lawn drenched with dew. It had been a heating walk, and I was glad to blunder on a garden seat, most considerately placed under a cedar which added its own darkness to that of the night. Here I rested a few minutes, putting up my feet to keep them dry, untying my shoes to save time, and generally facing the task before me with a coolness which I strove to make worthy of my absent chief. But mine was a self-conscious quality, as far removed from the original as any other deliberate imitation of genius. I actually struck a match on my trousers, and lit one of the shorter Sullivans. Raffles himself would not have done such a thing at such a moment. But I wished to tell him that I had done it; and in truth I was not more than pleasurably afraid; I had rather that impersonal curiosity as to the issue which has been the saving of me in still more precarious situations. I even grew impatient for the fray, and could not after all sit still as long as I had intended. So it happened that I was finishing my cigarette on the edge of the wet lawn, and about to slip off my shoes before stepping across the gravel to the conservatory door, when a most singular sound arrested me in the act. It was a muffled gasping somewhere overhead. I stood like stone; and my listening attitude must have been visible against the milky sheen of the lawn, for a labored voice hailed me sternly from a window.

"Who on earth are you?" it wheezed.

"A detective officer," I replied, "sent down by the Burglary Insurance Company."

Not a moment had I paused for my precious fable. It had all. been prepared for me by Raffles, in case of need. I was merely repeating a lesson in which I had been closely schooled. But at the window there was pause enough, filled only by the uncanny wheezing of the man I could not see.

"I don't see why they should have sent you down," he said at length. "We are being quite well looked after by the local police; they're giving us a special call every hour."

"I know that, Mr. Medlicott," I rejoined on my own account. "I met one of them at the corner just now, and we passed the time of night."

My heart was knocking me to bits. I had started for myself at last.

"Did you get my name from him?" pursued my questioner, in a suspicious wheeze.

"No; they gave me that before I started," I replied. "But I'm sorry you saw me, sir; it's a mere matter of routine, and not intended to annoy anybody. I propose to keep a watch on the place all. night, but I own it wasn't necessary to trespass as I've done. I'll take myself off the actual premises, if you prefer it."

This again was all. my own; and it met with a success that might have given me confidence.

"Not a bit of it," replied young Medlicott, with a grim geniality. "I've just woke up with the devil of an attack of asthma, and may have to sit up in my chair till morning. You'd better come up and see me through, and kill two birds while you're about it. Stay where you are, and I'll come down and let you in."

Here was a dilemma which Raffles himself had not foreseen! Outside, in the dark, my audacious part was not hard to play; but to carry the improvisation in-doors was to double at once the difficulty and the risk. It was true that I had purposely come down in a true detective's overcoat and bowler; but my personal appearance was hardly of the detective type. On the other hand as the soi-disant guardian of the gifts one might only excite suspicion by refusing to enter the house where they were. Nor could I forget that it was my purpose to effect such entry first or last. That was the casting consideration. I decided to take my dilemma by the horns.

There had been a scraping of matches in the room over the conservatory; the open window had shown for a moment, like an empty picture-frame, a gigantic shadow wavering on the ceiling; and in the next half-minute I remembered to tie my shoes. But the light was slow to reappear through the leaded glasses of an outer door farther along the path. And when the door opened, it was a figure of woe that stood within and held an unsteady candle between our faces.

I have seen old men look half their age, and young men look double theirs; but never before or since have I seen a beardless boy bent into a man of eighty, gasping for every breath, shaken by every gasp, swaying, tottering, and choking, as if about to die upon his feet. Yet with it all., young Medlicott overhauled me shrewdly, and it was several moments before he would let me take the candle from him.

"I shouldn't have come down—made me worse," he began whispering in spurts. "Worse still going up again. You must give me an arm. You will come up? That's right! Not as bad as I look, you know. Got some good whiskey, too.

Presents are all. right; but if they aren't you'll hear of it in-doors sooner than out. Now I'm ready—thanks! Mustn't make more noise than we can help—wake my mother."

It must have taken us minutes to climb that single flight of stairs. There was just room for me to keep his arm in mine; with the other he hauled on the banisters; and so we mounted, step by step, a panting pause on each, and a pitched battle for breath on the half-landing. In the end we gained a cosey library, with an open door leading to a bedroom beyond. But the effort had deprived my poor companion of all. power of speech; his laboring lungs shrieked like the wind; he could just point to the door by which we had entered, and which I shut in obedience to his gestures, and then to the decanter and its accessories on the table where he had left them overnight. I gave him nearly half a glassful, and his paroxysm subsided a little as he sat hunched up in a chair.

"I was a fool...to turn in," he blurted in more whispers between longer pauses. "Lying down is the devil...when you're in for a real bad night. You might get me the brown cigarettes...on the table in there. That's right...thanks awfully...and now a match!"

The asthmatic had bitten off either end of the stramonium cigarette, and was soon choking himself with the crude fumes, which he inhaled in desperate gulps, to exhale in furious fits of coughing. Never was more heroic remedy; it seemed a form of lingering suicide; but by degrees some slight improvement became apparent, and at length the sufferer was able to sit upright, and to drain his glass with a sigh of rare relief. I sighed also, for I had witnessed a struggle for dear life by a man in the flower of his youth, whose looks I liked, whose smile came like the sun through the first break in his torments, and whose first words were to thank me for the little I had done in bare humanity.

That made me feel the thing I was. But the feeling put me on my guard. And I was not unready for the remark which followed a more exhaustive scrutiny than I had hitherto sustained.

"Do you know," said young Medlicott, "that you aren't a bit like the detective of my dreams?"

"Only to proud to hear it," I replied. "There would be no point in my being in plain clothes if I looked exactly what I was."

My companion reassured me with a wheezy laugh.

"There's something in that," said he, "although I do congratulate the insurance people on getting a man of your class to do their dirty work. And I congratulate myself," he was quick enough to add, "on having you to see me through as bad a night as I've had for a long time. You're like flowers in the depths of winter. Got a drink? That's right! I suppose you didn't happen to bring down an evening paper?"

I said I had brought one, but had unfortunately left it in the train.

"What about the Test Match?" cried my asthmatic, shooting forward in his chair.

"I can tell you that," said I. "We went in first—"

"Oh, I know all. about that," he interrupted. "I've seen the miserable score up to lunch. How many did we scrape altogether?"

"We're scraping them still."

"No! How many?"

"Over two hundred for seven wickets."

"Who made the stand?"

"Raffles, for one. He was 62 not out at close of play!"

And the note of admiration rang in my voice, though I tried in my self-consciousness to keep it out. But young Medlicott's enthusiasm proved an ample cloak for mine; it was he who might have been the personal friend of Raffles; and in his delight he chuckled till he puffed and blew again.

"Good old Raffles!" he panted in every pause. "After being chosen last, and as a bowler-man! That's the cricketer for me, sir; by Jove, we must have another drink in his honor! Funny thing, asthma; your liquor affects your head no more than it does a man with a snake-bite; but it eases everything else, and sees you through. Doctors will tell you so, but you've got to ask 'em first; they're no good for asthma! I've only known one who could stop an attack, and he knocked me sideways with nitrite of amyl. Funny complaint in other ways; raises your spirits, if anything. You can't look beyond the next breath. Nothing else worries you. Well, well, here's luck to A. J. Raffles, and may he get his century in the morning!"

And he struggled to his feet for the toast; but I drank it sitting down. I felt unreasonably wroth with Raffles, for coming into the conversation as he had done—for taking centuries in Test Matches as he was doing, without bothering his head about me. A failure would have been in better taste; it would have shown at least some imagination, some anxiety on one's account I did not reflect that even Raffles could scarcely be expected to picture me in my cups with the son of the house that I had come to rob; chatting with him, ministering to him; admiring his cheery courage, and honestly attempting to lighten his load! Truly it was an infernal position: how could I rob him or his after this? And yet I had thrust myself into it; and Raffles would never, never understand!

Even that was not the worst. I was not quite sure that young Medlicott was sure of me. I had feared this from the beginning, and now (over the second glass that could not possibly affect a man in his condition) he practically admitted as much to me. Asthma was such a funny thing (he insisted) that it would not worry him a bit to discover that I had come to take the presents instead of to take care of them! I showed a sufficiently faint appreciation of the jest. And it was presently punished as it deserved, by the most violent paroxysm that had seized the sufferer yet: the fight for breath became faster and more furious, and the former weapons of no more avail. I prepared a cigarette, but the poor brute was too breathless to inhale. I poured out yet more whiskey, but he put it from him with a gesture.

"Amyl—get me amyl!" he gasped. "The tin on the table by my bed."

I rushed into his room, and returned with a little tin of tiny cylinders done up like miniature crackers in scraps of calico; the spent youth broke one in his handkerchief, in which he immediately buried his face. I watched him closely as a subtle odor reached my nostrils; and it was like the miracle of oil upon the billows. His shoulders rested from long travail; the stertorous gasping died away to a quick but natural respiration; and in the sudden cessation of the cruel contest, an uncanny stillness fell upon the scene. Meanwhile the hidden face had flushed to the ears, and, when at length it was raised to mine, its crimson calm was as incongruous as an optical illusion.

"It takes the blood from the heart," he murmured, "and clears the whole show for the moment. If it only lasted! But you can't take two without a doctor; one's quite enough to make you smell the brimstone.... I say, what's up? You're listening to something! If it's the policeman we'll have a word with him."

It was not the policeman; it was no out-door sound that I had caught in the sudden cessation of the bout for breath. It was a noise, a footstep, in the room below us. I went to the window and leaned out: right underneath, in the conservatory, was the faintest glimmer of a light in the adjoining room.

"One of the rooms where the presents are!" whispered Medlicott at my elbow. And as we withdrew together, I looked him in the face as I had not done all. night.

I looked him in the face like an honest man, for a miracle was to make me one once more. My knot was cut—my course inevitable. Mine, after all., to prevent the very thing that I had come to do! My gorge had long since risen at the deed; the unforeseen circumstances had rendered it impossible from the first; but now I could afford to recognize the impossibility, and to think of Raffles and the asthmatic alike without a qualm. I could play the game by them both, for it was one and the same game. I could preserve thieves' honor, and yet regain some shred of that which I had forfeited as a man!

So I thought as we stood face to face, our ears straining for the least movement below, our eyes locked in a common anxiety. Another muffled foot-fall—felt rather than heard—and we exchanged grim nods of simultaneous excitement. But by this time Medlicott was as helpless as he had been before; the flush had faded from his face, and his breathing alone would have spoiled everything. In dumb show I had to order him to stay where he was, to leave my man to me. And then it was that in a gusty whisper, with the same shrewd look that had disconcerted me more than once during our vigil, young Medlicott froze and fired my blood by turns.

"I've been unjust to you," he said, with his right hand in his dressing-gown pocket. "I thought for a bit—never mind what I thought—I soon saw I was wrong. But—I've had this thing in my pocket all. the time!"

And he would have thrust his revolver upon me as a peace-offering, but I would not even take his hand, as I tapped the life-preserver in my pocket, and crept out to earn his honest grip or to fall in the attempt. On the landing I drew Raffles's little weapon, slipped my right wrist through the leathern loop, and held it in readiness over my right shoulder. Then, down-stairs I stole, as Raffles himself had taught me, close to the wall, where the planks are nailed. Nor had I made a sound, to my knowledge; for a door was open, and a light was burning, and the light did not flicker as I approached the door. I clenched my teeth and pushed it open; and here was the veriest villain waiting for me, his little lantern held aloft.

"You blackguard!" I cried, and with a single thwack I felled the ruffian to the floor.

There was no question of a foul blow. He had been just as ready to pounce on me; it was simply my luck to have got the first blow home. Yet a fellow-feeling touched me with remorse, as I stood over the senseless body, sprawling prone, and perceived that I had struck an unarmed man. The lantern only had fallen from his hands; it lay on one side, smoking horribly; and a something in the reek caused me to set it up in haste and turn the body over with both hands.

Shall I ever forget the incredulous horror of that moment?

It was Raffles himself!

How it was possible, I did not pause to ask myself; if one man on earth could annihilate space and time, it was the man lying senseless at my feet; and that was Raffles, without an instant's doubt. He was in villainous guise, which I knew of old, now that I knew the unhappy wearer. His face was grimy, and dexterously plastered with a growth of reddish hair; his clothes were those in which he had followed cabs from the London termini; his boots were muffled in thick socks; and I had laid him low with a bloody scalp that filled my cup of horror. I groaned aloud as I knelt over him and felt his heart. And I was answered by a bronchial whistle from the door.

"Jolly well done!" cheered my asthmatical friend. "I heard the whole thing— only hope my mother didn't. We must keep it from her if we can."

I could have cursed the creature's mother from my full heart; yet even with my hand on that of Raffles, as I felt his feeble pulse, I told myself that this served him right. Even had I brained him, the fault had been his, not mine. And it was a characteristic, an inveterate fault, that galled me for all. my anguish: to trust and yet distrust me to the end, to race through England in the night, to spy upon me at his work—to do it himself after all.!

"Is he dead?" wheezed the asthmatic coolly.

"Not he," I answered, with an indignation that I dared not show.

"You must have hit him pretty hard," pursued young Medlicott, "but I suppose it was a case of getting first knock. And a good job you got it, if this was his," he added, picking up the murderous little life-preserver which poor Raffles had provided for his own destruction.

"Look here," I answered, sitting back on my heels. "He isn't dead, Mr. Medlicott, and I don't know how long he'll be as much as stunned. He's a powerful brute, and you're not fit to lend a hand. But that policeman of yours can't be far away. Do you think you could struggle out and look for him?"

"I suppose I am a bit better than I was," he replied doubtfully. "The excitement seems to have done me good. If you like to leave me on guard with my revolver, I'll undertake that he doesn't escape me."

I shook my head with an impatient smile.

"I should never hear the last of it," said I. "No, in that case all. I can do is to handcuff the fellow and wait till morning if he won't go quietly; and he'll be a fool if he does, while there's a fighting chance."

Young Medlicott glanced upstairs from his post on the threshold. I refrained from watching him too keenly, but I knew what was in his mind.

"I'll go," he said hurriedly. "I'll go as I am, before my mother is disturbed and frightened out of her life. I owe you something, too, not only for what you've done for me, but for what I was fool enough to think about you at the first blush. It's entirely through you that I feel as fit as I do for the moment. So I'll take your tip, and go just as I am, before my poor old pipes strike up another tune."

I scarcely looked up until the good fellow had turned his back upon the final tableau of watchful officer and prostrate prisoner and gone out wheezing into the night. But I was at the door to hear the last of him down the path and round the corner of the house. And when I rushed back into the room, there was Raffles sitting cross-legged on the floor, and slowly shaking his broken head as he stanched the blood.

"Et tu, Bunny!" he groaned. "Mine own familiar friend!"

"Then you weren't even stunned!" I exclaimed. "Thank God for that!"

"Of course I was stunned," he murmured, "and no thanks to you that I wasn't brained. Not to know me in the kit you've seen scores of times! You never looked at me, Bunny; you didn't give me time to open my mouth. I was going to let you run me in so prettily! We'd have walked off arm-in-arm; now it's as tight a place as ever we were in, though you did get rid of old blow-pipes rather nicely. But we shall have the devil's own run for our money!"

Raffles had picked himself up between his mutterings, and I had followed him to the door into the garden, where he stood busy with the key in the dark, having blown out his lantern and handed it to me. But though I followed Raffles, as my nature must, I was far too embittered to answer him again. And so it was for some minutes that might furnish forth a thrilling page, but not a novel one to those who know their Raffles and put up with me. Suffice it that we left a locked door behind us, and the key on the garden wall, which was the first of half a dozen that we scaled before dropping into a lane that led to a foot-bridge higher up the backwater. And when we paused upon the foot-bridge, the houses along the bank were still in peace and darkness.

Knowing my Raffles as I did, I was not surprised when he dived under one end of this bridge, and came up with his Inverness cape and opera hat, which he had hidden there on his way to the house. The thick socks were peeled from his patent-leathers, the ragged trousers stripped from an evening pair, bloodstains and Newgate fringe removed at the water's edge, and the whole sepulchre whited in less time than the thing takes to tell. Nor was that enough for Raffles, but he must alter me as well, by wearing my overcoat under his cape, and putting his Zingari scarf about my neck.

"And now," said he, "you may be glad to hear there's a 3:12 from Surbiton, which we could catch on all. fours. If you like we'll go separately, but I don't think there's the slightest danger now, and I begin to wonder what's happening to old blow-pipes."

So, indeed, did I, and with no small concern, until I read of his adventures (and our own) in the newspapers. It seemed that he had made a gallant spurt into the road, and there paid the penalty of his rashness by a sudden incapacity to move another inch. It had eventually taken him twenty minutes to creep back to locked doors, and another ten to ring up the inmates. His description of my personal appearance, as reported in the papers, is the only thing that reconciles me to the thought of his sufferings during that half-hour.

But at the time I had other thoughts, and they lay too deep for idle words, for to me also it was a bitter hour. I had not only failed in my self-sought task; I had nearly killed my comrade into the bargain. I had meant well by friend and foe in turn, and I had ended in doing execrably by both. It was not all. my fault, but I knew how much my weakness had contributed to the sum. And I must walk with the man whose fault it was, who had travelled two hundred miles to obtain this last proof of my weakness, to bring it home to me, and to make our intimacy intolerable from that hour. I must walk with him to Surbiton, but I need not talk; all. through Thames Ditton I had ignored his sallies; nor yet when he ran his arm through mine, on the river front, when we were nearly there, would I break the seal my pride had set upon my lips.

"Come, Bunny," he said at last, "I have been the one to suffer most, when all.'s said and done, and I'll be the first to say that I deserved it. You've broken my head; my hair's all. glued up in my gore; and what yarn I'm to put up at Manchester, or how I shall take the field at all., I really don't know. Yet I don't blame you, Bunny, and I do blame myself. Isn't it rather hard luck if I am to go unforgiven into the bargain? I admit that I made a mistake; but, my dear fellow, I made it entirely for your sake."

"For my sake!" I echoed bitterly.

Raffles was more generous; he ignored my tone.

"I was miserable about you—frankly—miserable!" he went on. "I couldn't get it out of my head that somehow you would be laid by the heels. It was not your pluck that I distrusted, my dear fellow, but it was your very pluck that made me tremble for you. I couldn't get you out of my head. I went in when runs were wanted, but I give you my word that I was more anxious about you; and no doubt that's why I helped to put on some runs. Didn't you see it in the paper, Bunny? It's the innings of my life, so far."

"Yes," I said, "I saw that you were in at close of play. But I don't believe it was you—I believe you have a double who plays your cricket for you!"

And at the moment that seemed less incredible than the fact.

"I'm afraid you didn't read your paper very carefully," said Raffles, with the first trace of pique in his tone. "It was rain that closed play before five o'clock. I hear it was a sultry day in town, but at Manchester we got the storm, and the ground was under water in ten minutes. I never saw such a thing in my life. There was absolutely not the ghost of a chance of another ball being bowled. But I had changed before I thought of doing what I did. It was only when I was on my way back to the hotel, by myself, because I couldn't talk to a soul for thinking of you, that on the spur of the moment I made the man take me to the station instead, and was under way in the restaurant car before I had time to think twice about it. I am not sure that of all. the mad deeds I have ever done, this was not the maddest of the lot!"

"It was the finest," I said in a low voice; for now I marvelled more at the impulse which had prompted his feat, and at the circumstances surrounding it, than even at the feat itself.

"Heaven knows," he went on, "what they are saying and doing in Manchester! But what can they say? 'What business is it of theirs? I was there when play stopped, and I shall be there when it starts again. We shall be at Waterloo just after half-past three, and that's going to give me an hour at the Albany on my way to Euston, and another hour at Old Trafford before play begins. What's the matter with that? I don't suppose I shall notch any more, but all. the better if I don't; if we have a hot sun after the storm, the sooner they get in the better; and may I have a bowl at them while the ground bites!"

"I'll come up with you," I said, "and see you at it."

"My dear fellow," replied Raffles, "that was my whole feeling about you. I wanted to 'see you at it'—that was absolutely all. I wanted to be near enough to lend a hand if you got tied up, as the best of us will at times. I knew the ground better than you, and I simply couldn't keep away from it. But I didn't mean you to know that I was there; if everything had gone as I hoped it might, I should have sneaked back to town without ever letting you know I had been up. You should never have dreamt that I had been at your elbow; you would have believed in yourself, and in my belief in you, and the rest would have been silence till the grave. So I dodged you at Waterloo, and I tried not to let you know that I was following you from Esher station. But you suspected somebody was; you stopped to listen more than once; after the second time I dropped behind, but gained on you by taking the short cut by Imber Court and over the foot-bridge where I left my coat and hat. I was actually in the garden before you were. I saw you smoke your Sullivan, and I was rather proud of you for it, though you must never do that sort of thing again. I heard almost every word between you and the poor devil upstairs. And up to a certain point, Bunny, I really thought you played the scene to perfection."

The station lights were twinkling ahead of us in the fading velvet of the summer's night. I let them increase and multiply before I spoke.

"And where," I asked, "did you think I first went wrong?"

"In going in-doors at all.," said Raffles. "If I had done that, I should have done exactly what you did from that point on. You couldn't help yourself, with that poor brute in that state. And I admired you immensely, Bunny, if that's any comfort to you now."

Comfort! It was wine in every vein, for I knew that Raffles meant what he said, and with his eyes I soon saw myself in braver colors. I ceased to blush for the vacillations of the night, since he condoned them. I could even see that I had behaved with a measure of decency, in a truly trying situation, now that Raffles seemed to think so. He had changed my whole view of his proceedings and my own, in every incident of the night but one. There was one thing, however, which he might forgive me, but which I felt that I could forgive neither Raffles nor myself. And that was the contused scalp wound over which I shuddered in the train.

"And to think that I did that," I groaned, "and that you laid yourself open to it, and that we have neither of us got another thing to show for our night's work! That poor chap said it was as bad a night as he had ever had in his life; but I call it the very worst that you and I ever had in ours."

Raffles was smiling under the double lamps of the first-class compartment that we had to ourselves.

"I wouldn't say that, Bunny. We have done worse."

"Do you mean to tell me that you did anything at all.?"

"My dear Bunny," replied Raffles, "you should remember how long I had been maturing felonious little plan, what a blow it was to me to have to turn it over to you, and how far I had travelled to see that you did it and yourself as well as might be. You know what I did see, and how well I understood. I tell you again that I should have done the same thing myself, in your place. But I was not in your place, Bunny. My hands were not tied like yours. Unfortunately, most of the jewels have gone on the honeymoon with the happy pair; but these emerald links are all. right, and I don't know what the bride was doing to leave this diamond comb behind. Here, too, is the old silver skewer I've been wanting for years—they make the most charming paper-knives in the world—and this gold cigarette-case will just do for your smaller Sullivans."

Nor were these the only pretty things that Raffles set out in twinkling array upon the opposite cushions. But I do not pretend that this was one of our heavy hauls, or deny that its chief interest still resides in the score of the Second Test Match of that Australian tour.

A Trap to Catch a Cracksman

I was just putting out my light when the telephone rang a furious tocsin in the next room. I flounced out of bed more asleep than awake; in another minute I should have been past ringing up. It was one o'clock in the morning, and I had been dining with Swigger Morrison at his club.

"Hulloa!"

"That you, Bunny?"

"Yes—are you Raffles?"

"What's left of me! Bunny, I want you—quick."

And even over the wire his voice was faint with anxiety and apprehension.

"What on earth has happened?"

"Don't ask! You never know—"

"I'll come at once. Are you there, Raffles?"

"What's that?"

"Are you there, man?"

"Ye—e—es."

"At the Albany?"

"No, no; at Maguire's."

"You never said so. And where's Maguire?"

"In Half-moon Street."

"I know that. Is he there now?"

"No—not come in yet—and I'm caught."

"Caught!"

"In that trap he bragged about. It serves me right. I didn't believe in it. But I'm caught at last...caught...at last!"

"When he told us he set it every night! Oh, Raffles, what sort of a trap is it? What shall I do? What shall I bring?"

But his voice had grown fainter and wearier with every answer, and now there was no answer at all. Again and again I asked Raffles if he was there; the only sound to reach me in reply was the low metallic hum of the live wire between his ear and mine. And then, as I sat gazing distractedly at my four safe walls, with the receiver still pressed to my head, there came a single groan, followed by the dull and dreadful crash of a human body falling in a heap.

In utter panic I rushed back into my bedroom, and flung myself into the crumpled shirt and evening clothes that lay where I had cast them off. But I knew no more what I was doing than what to do next I afterward found that I had taken out a fresh tie, and tied it rather better than usual; but I can remember thinking of nothing but Raffles in some diabolical man-trap, and of a grinning monster stealing in to strike him senseless with one murderous blow. I must have looked in the glass to array myself as I did; but the mind's eye was the seeing eye, and it was filled with this frightful vision of the notorious pugilist known to fame and infamy as Barney Maguire.

It was only the week before that Raffles and I had been introduced to him at the Imperial Boxing Club. Heavy-weight champion of the United States, the fellow was still drunk with his sanguinary triumphs on that side, and clamoring for fresh conquests on ours. But his reputation had crossed the Atlantic before Maguire himself; the grandiose hotels had closed their doors to him; and he had already taken and sumptuously furnished the house in Half-moon Street which does not re-let to this day. Raffles had made friends with the magnificent brute, while I took timid stock of his diamond studs, his jewelled watch-chain, his eighteen-carat bangle, and his six-inch lower jaw. I had shuddered to see Raffles admiring the gewgaws in his turn, in his own brazen fashion, with that air of the cool connoisseur which had its double meaning for me. I for my part would as lief have looked a tiger in the teeth. And when we finally went home with Maguire to see his other trophies, it seemed to me like entering the tiger's lair. But an astounding lair it proved, fitted throughout by one eminent firm, and ringing to the rafters with the last word on fantastic furniture.

The trophies were a still greater surprise. They opened my eyes to the rosier aspect of the noble art, as presently practised on the right side of the Atlantic. Among other offerings, we were permitted to handle the jewelled belt presented to the pugilist by the State of Nevada, a gold brick from the citizens of Sacramento, and a model of himself in solid silver from the Fisticuff Club in New York. I still remember waiting with bated breath for Raffles to ask Maguire if he were not afraid of burglars, and Maguire replying that he had a trap to catch the cleverest cracksman alive, but flatly refusing to tell us what it was. I could not at the moment conceive a more terrible trap than the heavy-weight himself behind a curtain. Yet it was easy to see that Raffles had accepted the braggart's boast as a challenge. Nor did he deny it later when I taxed him with his mad resolve; he merely refused to allow me to implicate myself in its execution. Well, there was a spice of savage satisfaction in the thought that Raffles had been obliged to turn to me in the end. And, but for the dreadful thud which I had heard over the telephone, I might have extracted some genuine comfort from the unerring sagacity with which he had chosen his night.

Within the last twenty-four hours Barney Maguire had fought his first great battle on British soil. Obviously, he would no longer be the man that he had been in the strict training before the fight; never, as I gathered, was such a ruffian more off his guard, or less capable of protecting himself and his possessions, than in these first hours of relaxation and inevitable debauchery for which Raffles had waited with characteristic foresight. Nor was the terrible Barney likely to be more abstemious for signal punishment sustained in a far from bloodless victory. Then what could be the meaning of that sickening and most suggestive thud? Could it be the champion himself who had received the coup de grace in his cups? Raffles was the very man to administer it—but he had not talked like that man through the telephone.

And yet—and yet—what else could have happened? I must have asked myself the question between each and all. of the above reflections, made partly as I dressed and partly in the hansom on the way to Half-moon Street. It was as yet the only question in my mind. You must know what your emergency is before you can decide how to cope with it; and to this day I sometimes tremble to think of the rashly direct method by which I set about obtaining the requisite information. I drove every yard of the way to the pugilist's very door. You will remember that I had been dining with Swigger Morrison at his club.

Yet at the last I had a rough idea of what I meant to say when the door was opened. It seemed almost probable that the tragic end of our talk over the telephone had been caused by the sudden arrival and as sudden violence of Barney Maguire. In that case I was resolved to tell him that Raffles and I had made a bet about his burglar trap, and that I had come to see who had won. I might or might not confess that Raffles had rung me out of bed to this end. If, however, I was wrong about Maguire, and he had not come home at all., then my action would depend upon the menial who answered my reckless ring. But it should result in the rescue of Raffles by hook or crook.

I had the more time to come to some decision, since I rang and rang in vain. The hall, indeed, was in darkness; but when I peeped through the letter-box I could see a faint beam of light from the back room. That was the room in which Maguire kept his trophies and set his trap. All. was quiet in the house: could they have haled the intruder to Vine Street in the short twenty minutes which it had taken me to dress and to drive to the spot? That was an awful thought; but even as I hoped against hope, and rang once more, speculation and suspense were cut short in the last fashion to be foreseen.

A brougham was coming sedately down the street from Piccadilly; to my horror, it stopped behind me as I peered once more through the letter-box, and out tumbled the dishevelled prizefighter and two companions. I was nicely caught in my turn. There was a lamp-post right opposite the door, and I can still see the three of them regarding me in its light. The pugilist had been at least a fine figure of a bully and a braggart when I saw him before his fight; now he had a black eye and a bloated lip, hat on the back of his head, and made-up tie under one ear. His companions were his sallow little Yankee secretary, whose name I really forget, but whom I met with Maguire at the Boxing Club, and a very grand person in a second skin of shimmering sequins.

I can neither forget nor report the terms in which Barney Maguire asked me who I was and what I was doing there. Thanks, however, to Swigger Morrison's hospitality, I readily reminded him of our former meeting, and of more that I only recalled as the words were in my mouth.

"You'll remember Raffles," said I, "if you don't remember me. You showed us your trophies the other night, and asked us both to look you up at any hour of the day or night after the fight."

I was going on to add that I had expected to find Raffles there before me, to settle a wager that we had made about the man-trap. But the indiscretion was interrupted by Maguire himself, whose dreadful fist became a hand that gripped mine with brute fervor, while with the other he clouted me on the back.

"You don't say!" he cried. "I took you for some darned crook, but now I remember you perfectly. If you hadn't've spoke up slick I'd have bu'st your face in, sonny. I would, sure! Come right in, and have a drink to show there's— Jeehoshaphat!"

The secretary had turned the latch-key in the door, only to be hauled back by the collar as the door stood open, and the light from the inner room was seen streaming upon the banisters at the foot of the narrow stairs.

"A light in my den," said Maguire in a mighty whisper, "and the blamed door open, though the key's in my pocket and we left it locked! Talk about crooks, eh? Holy smoke, how I hope we've landed one alive! You ladies and gentlemen, lay round where you are, while I see."

And the hulking figure advanced on tiptoe, like a performing elephant, until just at the open door, when for a second we saw his left revolving like a piston and his head thrown back at its fighting angle. But in another second his fists were hands again, and Maguire was rubbing them together as he stood shaking with laughter in the light of the open door.

"Walk up!" he cried, as he beckoned to us three. "Walk up and see one o' their blamed British crooks laid as low as the blamed carpet, and nailed as tight!"

Imagine my feelings on the mat! The sallow secretary went first; the sequins glittered at his heels, and I must own that for one base moment I was on the brink of bolting through the street door. It had never been shut behind us. I shut it myself in the end. Yet it was small credit to me that I actually remained on the same side of the door as Raffles.

"Reel home-grown, low-down, unwashed Whitechapel!" I had heard Maguire remark within. "Blamed if our Bowery boys ain't cock-angels to scum like this. Ah, you biter, I wouldn't soil my knuckles on your ugly face; but if I had my thick boots on I'd dance the soul out of your carcass for two cents!"

After this it required less courage to join the others in the inner room; and for some moments even I failed to identify the truly repulsive object about which I found them grouped. There was no false hair upon the face, but it was as black as any sweep's. The clothes, on the other hand, were new to me, though older and more pestiferous in themselves than most worn by Raffles for professional purposes. And at first, as I say, I was far from sure whether it was Raffles at all.; but I remembered the crash that cut short our talk over the telephone; and this inanimate heap of rags was lying directly underneath a wall instrument, with the receiver dangling over him.

"Think you know him?" asked the sallow secretary, as I stooped and peered with my heart in my boots.

"Good Lord, no! I only wanted to see if he was dead," I explained, having satisfied myself that it was really Raffles, and that Raffles was really insensible. "But what on earth has happened?" I asked in my turn.

"That's what I want to know," whined the person in sequins, who had contributed various ejaculations unworthy of report, and finally subsided behind an ostentatious fan.

"I should judge," observed the secretary, "that it's for Mr. Maguire to say, or not to say, just as he darn pleases."

But the celebrated Barney stood upon a Persian hearth-rug, beaming upon us all. in a triumph too delicious for immediate translation into words. The room was furnished as a study, and most artistically furnished, if you consider outlandish shapes in fumed oak artistic. There was nothing of the traditional prize-fighter about Barney Maguire, except his vocabulary and his lower jaw. I had seen over his house already, and it was fitted and decorated throughout by a high-art firm which exhibits just such a room as that which was the scene of our tragedietta. The person in the sequins lay glistening like a landed salmon in a quaint chair of enormous nails and tapestry compact. The secretary leaned against an escritoire with huge hinges of beaten metal. The pugilist's own background presented an elaborate scheme of oak and tiles, with inglenooks green from the joiner, and a china cupboard with leaded panes behind his bullet head. And his bloodshot eyes rolled with rich delight from the decanter and glasses on the octagonal table to another decanter in the quaintest and craftiest of revolving spirit tables.

"Isn't it bully?" asked the prize-fighter, smiling on us each in turn, with his black and bloodshot eyes and his bloated lip. "To think that I've only to invent a trap to catch a crook, for a blamed crook to walk right into! You, Mr. Man," and he nodded his great head at me, "you'll recollect me telling you that I'd gotten one when you come in that night with the other sport? Say, pity he's not with you now; he was a good boy, and I liked him a lot; but he wanted to know too much, and I guess he'd got to want. But I'm liable to tell you now, or else bu'st. See that decanter on the table?"

"I was just looking at it," said the person in sequins. "You don't know what a turn I've had, or you'd offer me a little something."

"You shall have a little something in a minute," rejoined Maguire. "But if you take a little anything out of that decanter, you'll collapse like our friend upon the floor."

"Good heavens!" I cried out, with involuntary indignation, and his fell scheme broke upon me in a clap.

"Yes, sir!" said Maguire, fixing me with his bloodshot orbs. "My trap for crooks and cracksmen is a bottle of hocussed whiskey, and I guess that's it on the table, with the silver label around its neck. Now look at this other decanter, without any label at all.; but for that they're the dead spit of each other. I'll put them side by side, so you can see. It isn't only the decanters, but the liquor looks the same in both, and tastes so you wouldn't know the difference till you woke up in your tracks. I got the poison from a blamed Indian away west, and it's ruther ticklish stuff. So I keep the label around the trap-bottle, and only leave it out nights. That's the idea, and that's all. there is to it," added Maguire, putting the labelled decanter back in the stand. "But I figure it's enough for ninety-nine crooks out of a hundred, and nineteen out of twenty 'll have their liquor before they go to work."

"I wouldn't figure on that," observed the secretary, with a downward glance as though at the prostrate Raffles. "Have you looked to see if the trophies are all. safe?"

"Not yet," said Maguire, with a glance at the pseudo-antique cabinet in which he kept them. "Then you can save yourself the trouble," rejoined the secretary, as he dived under the octagonal table, and came up with a small black bag that I knew at a glance. It was the one that Raffles had used for heavy plunder ever since I had known him.

The bag was so heavy now that the secretary used both hands to get it on the table. In another moment he had taken out the jewelled belt presented to Maguire by the State of Nevada, the solid silver statuette of himself, and the gold brick from the citizens of Sacramento.

Either the sight of his treasures, so nearly lost, or the feeling that the thief had dared to tamper with them after all., suddenly infuriated Maguire to such an extent that he had bestowed a couple of brutal kicks upon the senseless form of Raffles before the secretary and I could interfere.

"Play light, Mr. Maguire!" cried the sallow secretary. "The man's drugged, as well as down."

"He'll be lucky if he ever gets up, blight and blister him!"

"I should judge it about time to telephone for the police."

"Not till I've done with him. Wait till he comes to! I guess I'll punch his face into a jam pudding! He shall wash down his teeth with his blood before the coppers come in for what's left!"

"You make me feel quite ill," complained the grand lady in the chair. "I wish you'd give me a little something, and not be more vulgar than you can 'elp."

"Help yourself," said Maguire, ungallantly, "and don't talk through your hat. Say, what's the matter with the 'phone?"

The secretary had picked up the dangling receiver.

"It looks to me," said he, "as though the crook had rung up somebody before he went off."

I turned and assisted the grand lady to the refreshment that she craved.

"Like his cheek!" Maguire thundered. "But who in blazes should he ring up?"

"It'll all. come out," said the secretary. "They'll tell us at the central, and we shall find out fast enough."

"It don't matter now," said Maguire. "Let's have a drink and then rouse the devil up."

But now I was shaking in my shoes. I saw quite clearly what this meant. Even if I rescued Raffles for the time being, the police would promptly ascertain that it was I who had been rung up by the burglar, and the fact of my not having said a word about it would be directly damning to me, if in the end it did not incriminate us both. It made me quite faint to feel that we might escape the Scylla of our present peril and yet split on the Charybdis of circumstantial evidence. Yet I could see no middle course of conceivable safety, if I held my tongue another moment. So I spoke up desperately, with the rash resolution which was the novel feature of my whole conduct on this occasion. But any sheep would be resolute and rash after dining with Swigger Morrison at his club.

"I wonder if he rang me up?" I exclaimed, as if inspired.

"You, sonny?" echoed Maguire, decanter in hand. "What in hell could he know about you?"

"Or what could you know about him?" amended the secretary, fixing me with eyes like drills.

"Nothing," I admitted, regretting my temerity with all. my heart. "But some one did ring me up about an hour ago. I thought it was Raffles. I told you I expected to find him here, if you remember."

"But I don't see what that's got to do with the crook," pursued the secretary, with his relentless eyes boring deeper and deeper into mine.

"No more do I," was my miserable reply. But there was a certain comfort in his words, and some simultaneous promise in the quantity of spirit which Maguire splashed into his glass.

"Were you cut off sudden?" asked the secretary, reaching for the decanter, as the three of us sat round the octagonal table.

"So suddenly," I replied, "that I never knew who it was who rang me up. No, thank you—not any for me."

"What!" cried Maguire, raising a depressed head suddenly. "You won't have a drink in my house? Take care, young man. That's not being a good boy!"

"But I've been dining out," I expostulated, "and had my whack. I really have."

Barney Maguire smote the table with terrific

"Say, sonny, I like you a lot," said he. "But I shan't like you any if you're not a good boy!"

"Very well, very well," I said hurriedly. "One finger, if I must."

And the secretary helped me to not more than two.

"Why should it have been your friend Raffles?" he inquired, returning remorselessly to the charge, while Maguire roared "Drink up!" and then drooped once more.

"I was half asleep," I answered, "and he was the first person who occurred to me. We are both on the telephone, you see. And we had made a bet—"

The glass was at my lips, but I was able to set it down untouched. Maguire's huge jaw had dropped upon his spreading shirt-front, and beyond him I saw the person in sequins fast asleep in the artistic armchair.

"What bet?" asked a voice with a sudden start in it. The secretary was blinking as he drained his glass.

"About the very thing we've just had explained to us," said I, watching my man intently as I spoke. "I made sure it was a man-trap. Raffles thought it must be something else. We had a tremendous argument about it. Raffles said it wasn't a man-trap. I said it was. We had a bet about it in the end. I put my money on the man-trap. Raffles put his upon the other thing. And Raffles was right—it wasn't a man-trap. But it's every bit as good—every little bit—and the whole boiling of you are caught in it except me!"

I sank my voice with the last sentence, but I might just as well have raised it instead. I had said the same thing over and over again to see whether the wilful tautology would cause the secretary to open his eyes. It seemed to have had the very opposite effect. His head fell forward on the table, with never a quiver at the blow, never a twitch when I pillowed it upon one of his own sprawling arms.

And there sat Maguire bolt upright, but for the jowl upon his shirt-front, while the sequins twinkled in a regular rise and fall upon the reclining form of the lady in the fanciful chair. All. three were sound asleep, by what accident or by whose design I did not pause to inquire; it was enough to ascertain the fact beyond all. chance of error.

I turned my attention to Raffles last of all. There was the other side of the medal. Raffles was still sleeping as sound as the enemy—or so I feared at first I shook him gently: he made no sign. I introduced vigor into the process: he muttered incoherently. I caught and twisted an unresisting wrist—and at that he yelped profanely. But it was many and many an anxious moment before his blinking eyes knew mine.

"Bunny!" he yawned, and nothing more until his position came back to him. "So you came to me," he went on, in a tone that thrilled me with its affectionate appreciation, "as I knew you would! Have they turned up yet? They will any minute, you know; there's not one to lose."

"No, they won't, old man!" I whispered. And he sat up and saw the comatose trio for himself.

Raffles seemed less amazed at the result than I had been as a puzzled witness of the process; on the other hand, I had never seen anything quite so exultant as the smile that broke through his blackened countenance like a light. It was all. obviously no great surprise, and no puzzle at all., to Raffles.

"How much did they have, Bunny?" were his first whispered words.

"Maguire a good three fingers, and the others at least two."

"Then we needn't lower our voices, and we needn't walk on our toes. Eheu! I dreamed somebody was kicking me in the ribs, and I believe it must have been true."

He had risen with a hand to his side and a wry look on his sweep's face.

"You can guess which of them it was," said I. "The beast is jolly well served!"

And I shook my fist in the paralytic face of the most brutal bruiser of his time.

"He is safe till the forenoon, unless they bring a doctor to him," said Raffles. "I don't suppose we could rouse him now if we tried. How much of the fearsome stuff do you suppose I took? About a tablespoonful! I guessed what it was, and couldn't resist making sure; the minute I was satisfied, I changed the label and the position of the two decanters, little thinking I should stay to see the fun; but in another minute I could hardly keep my eyes open. I realized then that I was fairly poisoned with some subtle drug. If I left the house at all. in that state, I must leave the spoil behind, or be found drunk in the gutter with my head on the swag itself. In any case I should have been picked up and run in, and that might have led to anything."

"So you rang me up!"

"It was my last brilliant inspiration—a sort of flash in the brain-pan before the end—and I remember very little about it. I was more asleep than awake at the time."

"You sounded like it, Raffles, now that one has the clue."

"I can't remember a word I said, or what was the end of it, Bunny."

"You fell in a heap before you came to the end."

"You didn't hear that through the telephone?"

"As though we had been in the same room: only I thought it was Maguire who had stolen a march on you and knocked you out."

I had never seen Raffles more interested and impressed; but at this point his smile altered, his eyes softened, and I found my hand in his.

"You thought that, and yet you came like a shot to do battle for my body with Barney Maguire! Jack-the-Giant-killer wasn't in it with you, Bunny!"

"It was no credit to me—it was rather the other thing," said I, remembering my rashness and my luck, and confessing both in a breath. "You know old Swigger Morrison?" I added in final explanation. "I had been dining with him at his club!"

Raffles shook his long old head. And the kindly light in his eyes was still my infinite reward.

"I don't care," said he, "how deeply you had been dining: in vino veritas, Bunny, and your pluck would always out! I have never doubted it, and I never shall. In fact, I rely on nothing else to get us out of this mess."

My face must have fallen, as my heart sank at these words. I had said to myself that we were out of the mess already—that we had merely to make a clean escape from the house—now the easiest thing in the world. But as I looked at Raffles, and as Raffles looked at me, on the threshold of the room where the three sleepers slept on without sound or movement, I grasped the real problem that lay before us. It was twofold; and the funny thing was that I had seen both horns of the dilemma for myself, before Raffles came to his senses. But with Raffles in his right mind, I had ceased to apply my own, or to carry my share of our common burden another inch. It had been an unconscious withdrawal on my part, an instinctive tribute to my leader; but, I was sufficiently ashamed of it as we stood and faced the problem in each other's eyes.

"If we simply cleared out," continued Raffles, "you would be incriminated in the first place as my accomplice, and once they had you they would have a compass with the needle pointing straight to me. They mustn't have either of us, Bunny, or they will get us both. And for my part they may as well!"

I echoed a sentiment that was generosity itself in Raffles, but in my case a mere truism.

"It's easy enough for me," he went on. "I am a common house-breaker, and I escape. They don't know me from Noah. But they do know you; and how do you come to let me escape? What has happened to you, Bunny? That's the crux. What could have happened after they all. dropped off?" And for a minute Raffles frowned and smiled like a sensation novelist working out a plot; then the light broke, and transfigured him through his burnt cork. "I've got it, Bunny!" he exclaimed. "You took some of the stuff yourself, though of course not nearly so much as they did.

"Splendid!" I cried. "They really were pressing it upon me at the end, and I did say it must be very little."

"You dozed off in your turn, but you were naturally the first to come to yourself. I had flown; so had the gold brick, the jewelled belt, and the silver statuette. You tried to rouse the others. You couldn't succeed; nor would you if you did try. So what did you do? What's the only really innocent thing you could do in the circumstances?"

"Go for the police," I suggested dubiously, little relishing the prospect.

"There's a telephone installed for the purpose," said Raffles. "I should ring them up, if I were you. Try not to look blue about it, Bunny. They're quite the nicest fellows in the world, and what you have to tell them is a mere microbe to the camels I've made them swallow without a grain of salt. It's really the most convincing story one could conceive; but unfortunately there's another point which will take more explaining away."

And even Raffles looked grave enough as I nodded.

"You mean that they'll find out you rang me up?"

"They may," said Raffles. "I see that I managed to replace the receiver all. right. But still—they may."

"I'm afraid they will," said I, uncomfortably. "I'm very much afraid I gave something of the kind away. You see, you had not replaced the receiver; it was dangling over you where you lay. This very question came up, and the brutes themselves seemed so quick to see its possibilities that I thought best to take the bull by the horns and own that I had been rung up by somebody. To be absolutely honest, I even went so far as to say I thought it was Raffles!"

"You didn't, Bunny!"

"What could I say? I was obliged to think of somebody, and I saw they were not going to recognize you. So I put up a yarn about a wager we had made about this very trap of Maguire's. You see, Raffles, I've never properly told you how I got in, and there's no time now; but the first thing I had said was that I half expected to find you here before me. That was in case they spotted you at once. But it made all. that part about the telephone fit in rather well."

"I should think it did, Bunny," murmured Raffles, in a tone that added sensibly to my reward. "I couldn't have done better myself, and you will forgive my saying that you have never in your life done half so well. Talk about that crack you gave me on the head! You have made it up to me a hundredfold by all. you have done to-night. But the bother of it is that there's still so much to do, and to hit upon, and so precious little time for thought as well as action."

I took out my watch and showed it to Raffles without a word. It was three o'clock in the morning, and the latter end of March. In little more than an hour there would be dim daylight in the streets. Raffles roused himself from a reverie with sudden decision.

"There's only one thing for it, Bunny," said he. "We must trust each other and divide the labor. You ring up the police,(and leave the rest to me."

"You haven't hit upon any reason for the sort of burglar they think you were, ringing up the kind of man they know I am?"

"Not yet, Bunny, but I shall. It may not be wanted for a day or so, and after all. it isn't for you to give the explanation. It would be highly suspicious if you did."

"So it would," I agreed.

"Then will you trust me to hit on something—if possible before morning—in any case by the time it s wanted? I won't fail you, Bunny. You must see how I can never, never fail you after to-night!"

That settled it. I gripped his hand without another word, and remained on guard over the three sleepers while Raffles stole upstairs. I have since learned that there were servants at the top of the house, and in the basement a man, who actually heard some of our proceedings! But he was mercifully too accustomed to nocturnal orgies, and those of a far more uproarious character, to appear unless summoned to the scene. I believe he heard Raffles leave. But no secret was made of his exit: he let himself out and told me afterward that the first person he encountered in the street was the constable on the beat. Raffles wished him good-morning, as well he might; for he had been upstairs to wash his face and hands; and in the prize-fighter's great hat and fur coat he might have marched round Scotland Yard itself, in spite of his having the gold brick from Sacramento in one pocket, the silver statuette of Maguire in the other, and round his waist the jewelled belt presented to that worthy by the State of Nevada.

My immediate part was a little hard after the excitement of those small hours. I will only say that we had agreed that it would be wisest for me to lie like a log among the rest for half an hour, before staggering to my feet and rousing house and police; and that in that half-hour Barney Maguire crashed to the floor, without waking either himself or his companions, though not without bringing my beating heart into the very roof of my mouth.

It was daybreak when I gave the alarm with bell and telephone. In a few minutes we had the house congested with dishevelled domestics, irascible doctors, and arbitrary minions of the law. If I told my story once, I told it a dozen times, and all. on an empty stomach. But it was certainly a most plausible and consistent tale, even without that confirmation which none of the other victims was as yet sufficiently recovered to supply. And in the end I was permitted to retire from the scene until required to give further information, or to identify the prisoner whom the good police confidently expected to make before the day was out.

I drove straight to the flat. The porter flew to help me out of my hansom. His face alarmed me more than any I had left in Half-moon Street. It alone might have spelled my ruin.

"Your flat's been entered in the night, sir," he cried. "The thieves have taken everything they could lay hands on."

"Thieves in my flat!" I ejaculated aghast. There were one or two incriminating possessions up there, as well as at the Albany.

"The door's been forced with a jimmy," said the porter. "It was the milkman who found it out. There's a constable up there now."

A constable poking about in my flat of all. others! I rushed upstairs without waiting for the lift. The invader was moistening his pencil between laborious notes in a fat pocketbook; he had penetrated no further than the forced door. I dashed past him in a fever. I kept my trophies in a wardrobe drawer specially fitted with a Bramah lock. The lock was broken—the drawer void.

"Something valuable, sir?" inquired the intrusive constable at my heels.

"Yes, indeed—some old family silver," I answered. It was quite true. But the family was not mine.

And not till then did the truth flash across my mind. Nothing else of value had been taken. But there was a meaningless litter in all. the rooms. I turned to the porter, who had followed me up from the street; it was his wife who looked after the flat.

"Get rid of this idiot as quick as you can," I whispered. "I'm going straight to Scotland Yard myself. Let your wife tidy the place while I'm gone, and have the lock mended before she leaves. I'm going as I am, this minute!"

And go I did, in the first hansom I could find—but not straight to Scotland Yard. I stopped the cab in Picadilly on the way.

Old Raffles opened his own door to me. I cannot remember finding him fresher, more immaculate, more delightful to behold in every way. Could I paint a picture of Raffles with something other than my pen, it would be as I saw him that bright March morning, at his open door in the Albany, a trim, slim figure in matutinal gray, cool and gay and breezy as incarnate spring.

"What on earth did you do it for?" I asked within.

"It was the only solution," he answered, handing me the cigarettes. "I saw it the moment I got outside."

"I don't see it yet."

"Why should a burglar call an innocent gentleman away from home?"

"That's what we couldn't make out."

"I tell you I got it directly I had left you. He called you away in order to burgle you too, of course!"

And Raffles stood smiling upon me in all. his incomparable radiance and audacity.

"But why me?" I asked. "Why on earth should he burgle me?"

"My dear Bunny, we must leave something to the imagination of the police. But we will assist them to a fact or two in due season. It was the dead of night when Maguire first took us to his house; it was at the Imperial Boxing Club we met him; and you meet queer fish at the Imperial Boxing Club. You may remember that he telephoned to his man to prepare supper for us, and that you and he discussed telephones and treasure as we marched through the midnight streets. He was certainly bucking about his trophies, and for the sake of the argument you will be good enough to admit that you probably bucked about yours. What happens? You are overheard; you are followed; you are worked into the same scheme, and robbed on the same night."

"And you really think this will meet the case?"

"I am quite certain of it, Bunny, so far as it rests wit us to meet the case at all."

"Then give me another cigarette, my dear fellow, and let me push on to Scotland Yard."

Raffles held up both hands in admiring horror. "Scotland Yard!"

"To give a false description of what you took from that drawer in my wardrobe."

"A false description! Bunny, you have no more to learn from me. Time was when I wouldn't have let you go there without me to retrieve a lost umbrella— let alone a lost cause!"

And for once I was not sorry for Raffles to have the last unworthy word, as he stood once more at his outer door and gayly waved me down the stairs.

The Spoils of Sacrilege

There was one deed of those days which deserved a place in our original annals. It is the deed of which I am personally most ashamed. I have traced the course of a score of felonies, from their source in the brain of Raffles to their issue in his hands. I have omitted all. mention of the one which emanated from my own miserable mind. But in these supplementary memoirs, wherein I pledged myself to extenuate nothing more that I might have to tell of Raffles, it is only fair that I should make as clean a breast of my own baseness. It was I, then, and I alone, who outraged natural sentiment, and trampled the expiring embers of elementary decency, by proposing and planning the raid upon my own old home.

I would not accuse myself the more vehemently by making excuses at this point. Yet I feel bound to state that it was already many years since the place had passed from our possession into that of an utter alien, against whom I harbored a prejudice which was some excuse in itself. He had enlarged and altered the dear old place out of knowledge; nothing had been good enough for him as it stood in our day. The man was a hunting maniac, and where my dear father used to grow prize peaches under glass, this vandal was soon stabling his hothouse thoroughbreds, which took prizes in their turn at all. the country shows. It was a southern county, and I never went down there without missing another greenhouse and noting a corresponding extension to the stables. Not that I ever set foot in the grounds from the day we left; but for some years I used to visit old friends in the neighborhood, and could never resist the temptation to reconnoiter the scenes of my childhood. And so far as could be seen from the road—which it stood too near—the house itself appeared to be the one thing that the horsey purchaser had left much as he found it.

My only other excuse may be none at all. in any eyes but mine. It was my passionate desire at this period to "keep up my end" with Raffles in every department of the game felonious. He would insist upon an equal division of all. proceeds; it was for me to earn my share. So far I had been useful only at a pinch; the whole credit of any real success belonged invariably to Raffles. It had always been his idea. That was the tradition which I sought to end, and no means could compare with that of my unscrupulous choice. There was the one house in England of which I knew every inch, and Raffles only what I told him. For once I must lead, and Raffles follow, whether he liked it or not. He saw that himself; and I think he liked it better than he liked me for the desecration in view; but I had hardened my heart, and his feelings were too fine for actual remonstrance on such a point.

I, in my obduracy, went to foul extremes. I drew plans of all. the floors from memory. I actually descended upon my friends in the neighborhood, with the sole object of obtaining snap-shots over our own old garden wall. Even Raffles could not keep his eyebrows down when I showed him the prints one morning in the Albany. But he confined his open criticisms to the house.

"Built in the late 'sixties, I see," said Raffles, "or else very early in the 'seventies."

"Exactly when it was built," I replied. "But that's worthy of a sixpenny detective, Raffles! How on earth did you know?"

"That slate tower bang over the porch, with the dormer windows and the iron railing and flagstaff atop makes us a present of the period. You see them on almost every house of a certain size built about thirty years ago. They are quite the most useless excrescences I know."

"Ours wasn't," I answered, with some warmth. "It was my sanctum sanctorum in the holidays. I smoked my first pipe up there, and wrote my first verses."

Raffles laid a kindly hand upon my shoulder—"Bunny, Bunny, you can rob the old place, and yet you can't hear a word against it?"

"That's different," said I relentlessly. "The tower was there in my time, but the man I mean to rob was not."

"You really do mean to do it, Bunny?"

"By myself, if necessary? I averred.

"Not again, Bunny, not again," rejoined Raffles, laughing as he shook his head. "But do you think the man has enough to make it worth our while to go so far afield?"

"Far afield! It's not forty miles on the London and Brighton."

"Well, that's as bad as a hundred on most lines. And when did you say it was to be?"

"Friday week."

"I don't much like a Friday, Bunny. Why make it one?"

"It's the night of their Hunt Point-to-Point. They wind up the season with it every year; and the bloated Guillemard usually sweeps the board with his fancy flyers."

"You mean the man in your old house?"

"Yes; and he tops up with no end of dinner there," I went on, "to his hunting pals and the bloods who ride for him. If the festive board doesn't groan under a new regiment of challenge cups, it will be no fault of theirs, and old Guillemard will have to do them top-hole all. the same."

"So it's a case of common pot-hunting," remarked Raffles, eyeing me shrewdly through the cigarette smoke.

"Not for us, my dear fellow," I made answer in his own tone. "I wouldn't ask you to break into the next set of chambers here in the Albany for a few pieces of modern silver, Raffles. Not that we need scorn the cups if we get a chance of lifting them, and if Guillemard does so in the first instance. It's by no means certain that he will. But it is pretty certain to be a lively night for him and his pals—and a vulnerable one for the best bedroom!"

"Capital!" said Raffles, throwing coils of smoke between his smiles. "Still, if it's a dinner-party, the hostess won't leave her jewels upstairs. She'll wear them, my boy."

"Not all. of them, Raffles; she has far too many for that. Besides, it isn't an ordinary dinner-party; they say Mrs. Guillemard is generally the only lady there, and that she's quite charming in herself. Now, no charming woman would clap on all. sail in jewels for a roomful of fox-hunters."

"It depends what jewels she has."

"Well, she might wear her rope of pearls."

"I should have said so."

"And, of course, her rings."

"Exactly, Bunny."

"But not necessarily her diamond tiara—"

"Has she got one?"

"—and certainly not her emerald and diamond necklace on top of all.!"

Raffles snatched the Sullivan from his lips, and his eyes burned like its end.

"Bunny, do you mean to tell me there are all. these things?"

"Of course I do," said I. "They are rich people, and he's not such a brute as to spend everything on his stable. Her jewels are as much the talk as his hunters. My friends told me all. about both the other day when I was down making inquiries. They thought my curiosity as natural as my wish for a few snapshots of the old place. In their opinion the emerald necklace alone must be worth thousands of pounds."

Raffles rubbed his hands in playful pantomime.

"I only hope you didn't ask too many questions, Bunny! But if your friends are such old friends, you will never enter their heads when they hear what has happened, unless you are seen down there on the night, which might be fatal. Your approach will require some thought: if you like I can work out the shot for you. I shall go down independently, and the best thing may be to meet outside the house itself on the night of nights. But from that moment I am in your hands."

And on these refreshing lines our plan of campaign was gradually developed and elaborated into that finished study on which Raffles would rely like any artist of the footlights. None were more capable than he of coping with the occasion as it rose, of rising himself with the emergency of the moment, of snatching a victory from the very dust of defeat. Yet, for choice, every detail was premeditated, and an alternative expedient at each finger's end for as many bare and awful possibilities. In this case, however, the finished study stopped short at the garden gate or wall; there I was to assume command; and though Raffles carried the actual tools of trade of which he alone was master, it was on the understanding that for once I should control and direct their use.

I had gone down in evening-clothes by an evening train, but had carefully overshot old landmarks, and alighted at a small station some miles south of the one where I was still remembered. This committed me to a solitary and somewhat lengthy tramp; but the night was mild and starry, and I marched into it with a high stomach; for this was to be no costume crime, and yet I should have Raffles at my elbow all. the night. Long before I reached my destination, indeed, he stood in wait for me on the white highway, and we finished with linked arms.

"I came down early," said Raffles, "and had a look at the races. I always prefer to measure my man, Bunny; and you needn't sit in the front row of the stalls to take stock of your friend Guillemard. No wonder he doesn't ride his own horses! The steeple-chaser isn't foaled that would carry him round that course. But he's a fine monument of a man, and he takes his troubles in a way that makes me blush to add to them."

"Did he lose a horse?" I inquired cheerfully.

"No, Bunny, but he didn't win a race! His horses were by chalks the best there, and his pals rode them like the foul fiend, but with the worst of luck every time. Not that you'd think it, from the row they're making. I've been listening to them from the road—you always did say the house stood too near it."

"Then you didn't go in?"

"When it's your show? You should know me better. Not a foot would I set on the premises behind your back. But here they are, so perhaps you'll lead the way."

And I led it without a moment's hesitation, through the unpretentious six-barred gate into the long but shallow crescent of the drive. There were two such gates, one at each end of the drive, but no lodge at either, and not a light nearer than those of the house. The shape and altitude of the lighted windows, the whisper of the laurels on either hand, the very feel of the gravel underfoot, were at once familiar to my senses as the sweet, relaxing, immemorial air that one drank deeper at every breath. Our stealthy advance was to me like stealing back into one's childhood; and yet I could conduct it without compunction. I was too excited to feel immediate remorse, albeit not too lost in excitement to know that remorse for every step that I was taking would be my portion soon enough. I mean every word that I have written of my peculiar shame for this night's work. And it was all. to come over me before the night was out. But in the garden I never felt it once.

The dining-room windows blazed in the side of the house facing the road. That was an objection to peeping through the venetian blinds, as we nevertheless did, at our peril of observation from the road. Raffles would never have led me into danger so gratuitous and unnecessary, but he followed me into it without a word. I can only plead that we both had our reward. There was a sufficient chink in the obsolete venetians, and through it we saw every inch of the picturesque board. Mrs. Guillemard was still in her place, but she really was the only lady, and dressed as quietly as I had prophesied; round her neck was her rope of pearls, but not the glimmer of an emerald nor the glint of a diamond, nor yet the flashing constellation of a tiara in her hair. I gripped Raffles in token of my triumph, and he nodded as he scanned the overwhelming majority of flushed fox-hunters. With the exception of one stripling, evidently the son of the house, they were in evening pink to a man; and as I say, their faces matched their coats. An enormous fellow, with a great red face and cropped moustache, occupied my poor father's place; he it was who had replaced our fruitful vineries with his stinking stables; but I am bound to own he looked a genial clod, as he sat in his fat and listened to the young bloods boasting of their prowess, or elaborately explaining their mishaps. And for a minute we listened also, before I remembered my responsibilities, and led Raffles round to the back of the house.

There never was an easier house to enter. I used to feel that keenly as a boy, when, by a prophetic irony, burglars were my bugbear, and I looked under my bed every night in life. The bow-windows on the ground floor finished in inane balconies to the first-floor windows. These balconies had ornamental iron railings, to which a less ingenious rope-ladder than ours could have been hitched with equal ease. Raffles had brought it with him, round his waist, and he carried the telescopic stick for fixing it in place. The one was unwound, and the other put together, in a secluded corner of the red-brick walls, where of old I had played my own game of squash-rackets in the holidays. I made further investigations in the starlight, and even found a trace of my original white line along the red wall.

But it was not until we had effected our entry through the room which had been my very own, and made our parlous way across the lighted landing, to the best bedroom of those days and these, that I really felt myself a worm. Twin brass bedsteads occupied the site of the old four-poster from which I had first beheld the light. The doors were the same; my childish hands had grasped these very handles. And there was Raffles securing the landing door with wedge and gimlet, the very second after softly closing it behind us.

"The other leads into the dressing-room, of course? Then you might be fixing the outer dressing-room door," he whispered at his work, "but not the middle one Bunny, unless you want to. The stuff will be in there, you see, if it isn't in here."

My door was done in a moment, being fitted with a powerful bolt; but now an aching conscience made me busier than I need have been. I had raised the rope-ladder after us into my own old room, and while Raffles wedged his door I lowered the ladder from one of the best bedroom windows, in order to prepare that way of escape which was a fundamental feature of his own strategy. I meant to show Raffles that I had not followed in his train for nothing. But I left it to him to unearth the jewels. I had begun by turning up the gas; there appeared to be no possible risk in that; and Raffles went to work with a will in the excellent light. There were some good pieces in the room, including an ancient tallboy in fruity mahogany, every drawer of which was turned out on the bed without avail. A few of the drawers had locks to pick, yet not one triffle to our taste within. The situation became serious as the minutes flew. We had left the party at its sweets; the solitary lady might be free to roam her house at any minute. In the end we turned our attention to the dressing-room. And no sooner did Raffles behold the bolted door than up went his hands.

"A bathroom bolt," he cried below his breath, "and no bath in the room! Why didn't you tell me, Bunny? A bolt like that speaks volumes; there's none on the bedroom door, remember, and this one's worthy of a strong room! What if it is their strong room, Bunny! Oh, Bunny, what if this is their safe?"

Raffles had dropped upon his knees before a carved oak chest of indisputable antiquity. Its panels were delightfully irregular, its angles faultlessly faulty, its one modern defilement a strong lock to the lid. Raffles was smiling as he produced his jimmy. R—r—r—rip went lock or lid in another ten seconds— I was not there to see which. I had wandered back into the bedroom in a paroxysm of excitement and suspense. I must keep busy as well. as Raffles, and it was not too soon to see whether the rope-ladder was all. right. In another minute . . .

I stood frozen to the floor. I had hooked the ladder beautifully to the inner sill of wood, and had also let down the extended rod for the more expeditious removal of both on our return to terra firma. Conceive my cold horror on arriving at the open window just in time to see the last of hooks and bending rod, as they floated out of sight and reach into the outer darkness of the night, removed by some silent and invisible hand below!

"Raffles-Raffles—they've spotted us and moved the ladder this very instant!"

So I panted as I rushed on tiptoe to the dressing-room. Raffles had the working end of his jimmy under the lid of a leathern jewel case. It flew open at the vicious twist of his wrist that preceded his reply.

"Did you let them see that you'd spotted that?"

"No."

"Good! Pocket some of these cases—no time to open them. Which door's nearest the backstairs?"

"The other."

"Come on then?"

"No, no, I'll lead the way. I know every inch of it."

And, as I leaned against the bedroom door, handle in hand, while Raffles stooped to unscrew the gimlet and withdraw the wedge, I hit upon the ideal port in the storm that was evidently about to burst on our devoted heads. It was the last place in which they would look for a couple of expert cracksmen with no previous knowledge of the house. If only we could gain my haven unobserved, there we might lie in unsuspected hiding, and by the hour, if not for days and nights.

Alas for that sanguine dream! The wedge was out, and Raffles on his feet behind me. I opened the door, and for a second the pair of us stood upon the threshold.

Creeping up the stairs before us, each on the tip of his silken toes, was a serried file of pink barbarians, redder in the face than anywhere else, and armed with crops carried by the wrong end. The monumental person with the short moustache led the advance. The fool stood still upon the top step to let out the loudest and cheeriest view-holloa that ever smote my ears.

It cost him more than he may know until I tell him. There was the wide part of the landing between us; we had just that much start along the narrow part, with the walls and doors upon our left, the banisters on our right, and the baize door at the end. But if the great Guillemard had not stopped to live up to his sporting reputation, he would assuredly have laid one or other of us by the heels, and either would have been tantamount to both. As I gave Raffles a headlong lead to the baize door, I glanced down the great well of stairs, and up came the daft yells of these sporting oafs:

"Gone away—gone away!"

"Yoick—yoick—yoick?"

"Yon-der they go?"

And gone I had, through the baize door to the back landing, with Raffles at my heels. I held the swing door for him, and heard him bang it in the face of the spluttering and blustering master of the house. Other feet were already in the lower flight of the backstairs; but the upper flight was the one for me, and in an instant we were racing along the upper corridor with the chuckle-headed pack at our heels. Here it was all. but dark—they were the servants' bedrooms that we were passing now—but I knew what I was doing. Round the last corner to the right, through the first door to the left and we were in the room underneath the tower. In our time a long stepladder had led to the tower itself. I rushed in the dark to the old corner. Thank God, the ladder was there still! It leaped under us as we rushed aloft like one quadruped. The breakneck trap-door was still protected by a curved brass stanchion; this I grasped with one hand, and then Raffles with the other as I felt my feet firm upon the tower floor. In he sprawled after me, and down went the trap-door with a bang upon the leading hound.

I hoped to feel his dead-weight shake the house, as he crashed upon the floor below; but the fellow must have ducked, and no crash came. Meanwhile not a word passed between Raffles and me; he had followed me, as I had led him, without waste of breath upon a single syllable. But the merry lot below were still yelling and bellowing in full cry.

"Gone to ground? screamed one.

"Where's the terrier?" screeched another.

But their host of the mighty girth—a man like a soda-water bottle, from my one glimpse of him on his feet—seemed sobered rather than stunned by the crack on that head of his. We heard his fine voice no more, but we could feel him straining every thew against the trap-door upon which Raffles and I stood side by side. At least I thought Raffles was standing, until he asked me to strike a light, when I found him on his knees instead of on his feet, busy screwing down the trap-door with his gimlet. He carried three or four gimlets for wedging doors, and he drove them all. in to the handle, while I pulled at the stanchion and pushed with my feet.

But the upward pressure ceased before our efforts. We heard the ladder creak again under a ponderous and slow descent; and we stood upright in the dim flicker of a candle-end that I had lit and left burning on the floor. Raffles glanced at the four small windows in turn and then at me. "Is there any way out at all.?" he whispered, as no other being would or could have whispered to the man who had led him into such a trap. "We've no rope-ladder, you know."

"Thanks to me," I groaned. "The whole thing's my fault?

"Nonsense, Bunny; there was no other way to run. But what about these windows?"

His magnanimity took me by the throat; without a word I led him to the one window looking inward upon sloping slates and level leads. Often as a boy I had clambered over them, for the fearful fun of risking life and limb, or the fascination of peering through the great square skylight, down the well of the house into the hall below. There were, however, several smaller skylights, for the benefit of the top floor, through any one of which I thought we might have made a dash. But at a glance I saw we were too late: one of these skylights became a brilliant square before our eyes; opened, and admitted a flushed face on flaming shoulders.

"I'll give them a fright!" said Raffles through his teeth. In an instant he had plucked out his revolver, smashed the window with its butt, and the slates with a bullet not a yard from the protruding head. And that, I believe, was the only shot that Raffles ever fired in his whole career as a midnight marauder.

"You didn't hit him?" I gasped, as the head disappeared, and we heard a crash in the corridor.

"Of course I didn't, Bunny," he replied, backing into the tower; "but no one will believe I didn't mean to, and it'll stick on ten years if we're caught. That's nothing, if it gives us an extra five minutes now, while they hold a council of war. Is that a working flag-staff overhead?"

"It used to be."

"Then there'll be halliards."

"They were as thin as clothes-lines.".

"And they're sure to be rotten, and we should be seen cutting them down. No, Bunny, that won't do. Wait a bit. Is there a lightning conductor?"

"There was."

I opened one of the side windows and reached out as far as I could.

xyz

"You'll be seen from that skylight? cried Raffles in a warning undertone.

"No, I won't. I can't see it myself. But here's the lightning-conductor, where it always was."

"How thick," asked Raffles, as I drew in and rejoined him.

"Rather thicker than a lead-pencil."

"They sometimes bear you," said Raffles, slipping on a pair of white kid gloves, and stuffing his handkerchief into the palm of one. "The difficulty is to keep a grip; but I've been up and down them before to-night. And it's our only chance. I'll go first, Bunny: you watch me, and do exactly as I do if I get down all. right."

"But if you don't?"

"If I don't," whispered Raffles, as he wormed through the window feet foremost, "I'm afraid you'll have to face the music where you are, and I shall have the best of it down in Acheron!"

And he slid out of reach without another word, leaving me to shudder alike at his levity and his peril; nor could I follow him very far by the wan light of the April stars; but I saw his forearms resting a moment in the spout that ran around the tower, between bricks and slates, on the level of the floor; and I had another dim glimpse of him lower still, on the eaves over the very room that we had ransacked. Thence the conductor ran straight to earth in an angle of the facade. And since it had borne him thus far without mishap, I felt that Raffles was as good as down. But I had neither his muscles nor his nerves, and my head swam as I mounted to the window and prepared to creep out backward in my turn.

So it was that at the last moment I had my first unobstructed view of the little old tower of other days. Raffles was out of the way; the bit of candle was still burning on the floor, and in its dim light the familiar haunt was cruelly like itself of innocent memory. A lesser ladder still ascended to a tinier trap-door in the apex of the tower; the fixed seats looked to me to be wearing their old, old coat of grained varnish; nay the varnish had its ancient smell, and the very vanes outside creaked their message to my ears. I remembered whole days that I had spent, whole books that I had read, here in this favorite fastness of my boyhood. The dirty little place, with the dormer window in each of its four sloping sides, became a gallery hung with poignant pictures of the past. And here was I leaving it with my life in my hands and my pockets full of stolen jewels! A superstition seized me. Suppose the conductor came down with me . . . suppose I slipped . . . and was picked up dead, with the proceeds of my shameful crime upon me, under the very windows

> . . . where the sun
> Came peeping in at dawn . . .

I hardly remember what I did or left undone. I only know that nothing broke, that somehow I kept my hold, and that in the end the wire ran red-hot through my palms so that both were torn and bleeding when I stood panting beside Raffles in the flower-beds. There was no time for thinking then. Already there was a fresh commotion in-doors; the tidal wave of excitement which had swept all. before it to the upper regions was subsiding in as swift a rush downstairs; and I raced after Raffles along the edge of the drive without daring to look behind.

We came out by the opposite gate to that by which we had stolen in. Sharp to the right ran the private lane behind the stables and sharp to the right dashed Raffles, instead of straight along the open road. It was not the course I should have chosen, but I followed Raffles without a murmur, only too thankful that he had assumed the lead at last. Already the stables were lit up like a chandelier; there was a staccato rattle of horseshoes in the stable yard, and the great gates were opening as we skimmed past in the nick of time. In another minute we were skulking in the shadow of the kitchen-garden wall while the high-road rang with the dying tattoo of galloping hoofs.

"That's for the police," said Raffles, waiting for me. "But the fun's only beginning in the stables. Hear the uproar, and see the lights! In another minute they'll be turning out the hunters for the last run of the season

"We mustn't give them one, Raffles?"

"Of course we mustn't; but that means stopping where we are."

"We can't do that?"

"If they're wise they'll send a man to every railway station within ten miles and draw every cover inside the radius. I can only think of one that's not likely to occur to them."

"What's that?"

"The other side of this wall. How big is the garden, Bunny?"

"Six or seven acres."

"Well, you must take me to another of your old haunts, where we can lie low till morning."

"And then?"

"Sufficient for the night, Bunny! The first thing is to find a burrow. What are those trees at the end of this lane?"

"St. Leonard's Forest."

"Magnificent! They'll scour every inch of that before they come back to their own garden. Come, Bunny, give me a leg up, and I'll pull you after me in two ticks?

There was indeed nothing better to be done; and, much as I loathed and dreaded entering the place again, I had already thought of a second sanctuary of old days, which might as well be put to the base uses of this disgraceful night. In a far corner of the garden, over a hundred yards from the house, a little ornamental lake had been dug within my own memory; its shores were shelving lawn and steep banks of rhododendrons; and among the rhododendrons nestled a tiny boathouse which had been my childish joy. It was half a dock for the dingy in which one plowed these miniature waters and half a bathing-box for those who preferred their morning tub among the goldfish. I could not think of a safer asylum than this, if we must spend the night upon the premises; and Raffles agreed with me when I had led him by sheltering shrubbery and perilous lawn to the diminutive chalet between the rhododendrons and the water.

But what a night it was! The little bathing-box had two doors, one to the water, the other to the path. To hear all that could be heard, it was necessary to keep both doors open, and quite imperative not to talk. The damp night air of April filled the place, and crept through our evening clothes and light overcoats into the very marrow; the mental torture of the situation was renewed and multiplied in my brain; and all the time one's ears were pricked for footsteps on the path between the rhododendrons. The only sounds we could at first identify came one and all from the stables. Yet there the excitement subsided sooner than we had expected, and it was Raffles himself who breathed a doubt as to whether they were turning out the hunters after all. On the other hand, we heard wheels in the drive not long after midnight; and Raffles, who was beginning to scout among the shrubberies, stole back to tell me that the guests were departing, and being sped, with an unimpaired conviviality which he failed to understand. I said I could not understand it either, but suggested the general influence of liquor, and expressed my envy of their state. I had drawn my knees up to my chin, on the bench where one used to dry one's self after bathing, and there I sat in a seeming stolidity at utter variance with my inward temper. I heard

Raffles creep forth again and I let him go without a word. I never doubted that he would be back again in a minute, and so let many minutes elapse before I realized his continued absence, and finally crept out myself to look for him.

Even then I only supposed that he had posted himself outside in some more commanding position. I took a catlike stride and breathed his name. There was no answer. I ventured further, till I could overlook the lawns: they lay like clean slates in the starlight: there was no sign of living thing nearer than the house, which was still lit up, but quiet enough now. Was it a cunning and deliberate quiet assumed as a snare? Had they caught Raffles, and were they waiting for me? I returned to the boat-house in an agony of fear and indignation. It was fear for the long hours that I sat there waiting for him; it was indignation when at last I heard his stealthy step upon the gravel. I would not go out to meet him. I sat where I was while the stealthy step came nearer, nearer; and there I was sitting when the door opened, and a huge man in riding-clothes stood before me in the steely dawn.

I leaped to my feet, and the huge man clapped me playfully on the shoulder.

"Sorry I've been so long, Bunny, but we should never have got away as we were; this riding-suit makes a new man of me, on top of my own, and here's a youth's kit that should do you down to the ground."

"So you broke into the house again?

"I was obliged to, Bunny; but I had to watch the lights out one by one, and give them a good hour after that I went through that dressing room at my leisure this time; the only difficulty was to spot the son's quarters at the back of the house; but I overcame it, as you see, in the end. I only hope they'll fit, Bunny. Give me your patent leathers, and I'll fill them with stones and sink them in the pond. I'm doing the same with mine. Here's a brown pair apiece, and we mustn't let the grass grow under them if we're to get to the station in time for the early train while the coast's still clear."

The early train leaves the station in question at 6.20 A.M.; and that fine spring morning there was a police officer in a peaked cap to see it off; but he was too busy peering into the compartments for a pair of very swell mobsmen that he took no notice of the huge man in riding-clothes, who was obviously intoxicated, or the more insignificant but not less horsy character who had him in hand. The early train is due at Victoria at 8.28, but these worthies left it at Clapham Junction, and changed cabs more than once between Battersea and Piccadilly, and a few of their garments in each four-wheeler. It was barely nine o'clock when they sat together in the Albany, and might have been recognized once more as Raffles and myself.

"And now," said Raffles, "before we do anything else, let us turn out those little cases that we hadn't time to open when we took them. I mean the ones I handed to you, Bunny. I had a look into mine in the garden, and I'm sorry to say there was nothing in them. The lady must have been wearing their proper contents."

Raffles held out his hand for the substantial leather cases which I had produced at his request. But that was the extent of my compliance; instead of handing them over, I looked boldly into the eyes that seemed to have discerned my wretched secret at one glance.

"It is no use my giving them to you," I said. "They are empty also."

"When did you look into them?"

"In the tower."

"Well, let me see for myself."

"As you like."

"My dear Bunny, this one must have contained the necklace you boasted about."

"Very likely."

"And this one the tiara."

"I dare say."

"Yet she was wearing neither, as you prophesied, and as we both saw for ourselves?

I had not taken my eyes from his.

"Raffles," I said, "I'll be frank with you after all. I meant you never to know, but it's easier than telling you a lie. I left both things behind me in the tower. I won't attempt to explain or defend myself; it was probably the influence of the tower, and nothing else; but the whole thing came over me at the last moment, when you had gone and I was going. I felt that I should very probably break my neck, that I cared very little whether I did or not, but that it would be frightful to break it at that house with those things in my pocket. You may say I ought to have thought of all. that before! you may say what you like, and you won't say more than I deserve. It was hysterical, and it was mean, for I kept the cases to impose on you."

"You were always a bad liar, Bunny," said Raffles, smiling. "Will you think me one when I tell you that I can understand what you felt, and even what you did? As a matter of fact, I have understood for several hours now."

"You mean what I felt, Raffles?"

"And what you did. I guessed it in the boathouse. I knew that something must have happened or been discovered to disperse that truculent party of sportsmen so soon and on such good terms with themselves. They had not got us; they might have got something better worth having; and your phlegmatic attitude suggested what. As luck would have it, the cases that I personally had collared were the empty ones; the two prizes had fallen to you. Well, to allay my horrid suspicion, I went and had another peep through the lighted venetians. And what do you think I saw?"

I shook my head. I had no idea, nor was I very eager for enlightenment.

"The two poor people whom it was your own idea to despoil," quoth Raffles, "prematurely gloating over these two pretty things?

He withdrew a hand from either pocket of his crumpled dinner-jacket, and opened the pair under my nose. In one was a diamond tiara, and in the other a necklace of fine emeralds set in clusters of brilliants.

"You must try to forgive me, Bunny," continued Raffles before I could speak. "I don't say a word against what you did, or undid; in fact, now it's all.

over, I am rather glad to think that you did try to undo it. But, my dear fellow, we had both risked life, limb, and liberty; and I had not your sentimental scruples. Why should I go empty away? If you want to know the inner history of my second visit to that good fellow's dressing-room, drive home for a fresh kit and meet me at the Turkish bath in twenty minutes. I feel more than a little grubby, and we can have our breakfast in the cooling gallery. Besides, after a whole night in your old haunts, Bunny, it's only in order to wind up in Northumberland Avenue."

The Raffles Relics

It was in one of the magazines for December, 1899, that an article appeared which afforded our minds a brief respite from the then consuming excitement of the war in South Africa. These were the days when Raffles really had white hair, and when he and I were nearing the end of our surreptitious second innings, as professional cracksmen of the deadliest dye. Piccadilly and the Albany knew us no more. But we still operated, as the spirit tempted us, from our latest and most idyllic base, on the borders of Ham Common. Recreation was our greatest want; and though we had both descended to the humble bicycle, a lot of reading was forced upon us in the winter evenings. Thus the war came as a boon to us both. It not only provided us with an honest interest in life, but gave point and zest to innumerable spins across Richmond Park, to the nearest paper shop; and it was from such an expedition that I returned with inflammatory matter unconnected with the war. The magazine was one of those that are read (and sold) by the million; the article was rudely illustrated on every other page. Its subject was the so-called Black Museum at Scotland Yard; and from the catchpenny text we first learned that the gruesome show was now enriched by a special and elaborate exhibit known as the Raffles Relics.

"Bunny," said Raffles, "this is fame at last! It is no longer notoriety; it lifts one out of the ruck of robbers into the society of the big brass gods, whose little delinquencies are written in water by the finger of time. The Napoleon Relics we know, the Nelson Relics we've heard about, and here are mine!"

"Which I wish to goodness we could see," I added, longingly. Next moment I was sorry I had spoken. Raffles was looking at me across the magazine. There was a smile on his lips that I knew too well, a light in his eyes that I had kindled.

"What an excellent idea? he exclaimed, quite softly, as though working it out already in his brain.

"I didn't mean it for one," I answered, "and no more do you."

"Certainly I do," said Raffles. "I was never more serious in my life."

"You would march into Scotland Yard in broad daylight?"

"In broad lime-light," he answered, studying the magazine again, "to set eyes on my own once more. Why here they all. are, Bunny—you never told me there was an illustration. That's the chest you took to your bank with me inside, and those must be my own rope-ladder and things on top. They produce so badly in the baser magazines that it's impossible to swear to them; there's nothing for it but a visit of inspection."

"Then you can pay it alone," said I grimly. "You may have altered, but they'd know me at a glance."

"By all. means, Bunny, if you'll get me the pass."

"A pass? I cried triumphantly. "Of course we should have to get one, and of course that puts an end to the whole idea. Who on earth would give a pass for this show, of all. others, to an old prisoner like me?"

Raffles addressed himself to the reading of the magazine with a shrug that showed some temper.

"The fellow who wrote this article got one," said he shortly. "He got it from his editor, and you can get one from yours if you tried. But pray don't try, Bunny: it would be too terrible for you to risk a moment's embarrassment to gratify a mere whim of mine. And if I went instead of you and got spotted, which is so likely with this head of hair, and the general belief in my demise, the consequences to you would be too awful to contemplate! Don't contemplate them, my dear fellow. And do let me read my magazine."

Need I add that I set about the rash endeavor without further expostulation? I was used to such ebullitions from the altered Raffles of these later days, and I could well understand them. All. the inconvenience of the new conditions fell on him. I had purged my known offences by imprisonment, whereas Raffles was merely supposed to have escaped punishment in death. The result was that I could rush in where Raffles feared to tread, and was his plenipotentiary in all. honest dealings with the outer world. It could not but gall him to be so dependent upon me, and it was for me to minimize the humiliation by scrupulously avoiding the least semblance of an abuse of that power which I now had over him. Accordingly, though with much misgiving, I did his ticklish behest in Fleet Street, where, despite my past, I was already making a certain lowly footing for myself. Success followed as it will when one longs to fail; and one fine evening I returned to Ham Common with a card from the Convict Supervision Office, New Scotland Yard, which I treasure to this day. I am surprised to see that it was undated, and might still almost "Admit Bearer to see the Museum," to say nothing of the bearer's friends, since my editor's name "and party" is scrawled beneath the legend.

"But he doesn't want to come," as I explained to Raffles. "And it means that we can both go, if we both like."

Raffles looked at me with a wry smile; he was in good enough humor now.

"It would be rather dangerous, Bunny. If they spotted you, they might think of me."

"But you say they'll never know you now."

"I don't believe they will. I don't believe there's the slightest risk; but we shall soon see. I've set my heart on seeing, Bunny, but there's no earthly reason why I should drag you into it."

"You do that when you present this card," I pointed out. "I shall hear of it fast enough if anything happens."

"Then you may as well be there to see the fun?"

"It will make no difference if the worst comes to the worst."

"And the ticket is for a party, isn't it?"

"It is."

"It might even look peculiar if only one person made use of it?"

"It might."

"Then we're both going, Bunny! And I give you my word," cried Raffles, "that no real harm shall come of it. But you mustn't ask to see the Relics, and you mustn't take too much interest in them when you do see them. Leave the questioning to me: it really will be a chance of finding out whether they've any suspicion of one's resurrection at Scotland Yard. Still I think I can promise you a certain amount of fun, old fellow, as some little compensation for your pangs and fears?

The early afternoon was mild and hazy, and unlike winter but for the prematurely low sun struggling through the haze, as Raffles and I emerged from the nether regions at Westminster Bridge, and stood for one moment to admire the infirm silhouettes of Abbey and Houses in flat gray against a golden mist. Raffles murmured of Whistler and of Arthur Severn, and threw away a good Sullivan because the smoke would curl between him and the picture. It is perhaps the picture that I can now see clearest of all. the set scenes of our lawless life. But at the time I was filled with gloomy speculation as to whether Raffles would keep his promise of providing an entirely harmless entertainment for my benefit at the Black Museum.

We entered the forbidding precincts; we looked relentless officers in the face, and they almost yawned in ours as they directed us through swing doors and up stone stairs. There was something even sinister in the casual character of our reception. We had an arctic landing to ourselves for several minutes, which Raffles spent in an instinctive survey of the premises, while I cooled my heels before the portrait of a late commissioner.

"Dear old gentleman? exclaimed Raffles, joining me. "I have met him at dinner, and discussed my own case with him, in the old days. But we can't know too little about ourselves in the Black Museum, Bunny. I remember going to the old place in Whitehall, years ago, and being shown round by one of the tip-top 'tecs. And this may be another."

But even I could see at a glance that there was nothing of the detective and everything of the clerk about the very young man who had joined us at last upon the landing. His collar was the tallest I have ever seen, and his face was as pallid as his collar. He carried a loose key, with which he unlocked a door a little way along the passage, and so ushered us into that dreadful repository which perhaps has fewer visitors than any other of equal interest in the world. The place was cold as the inviolate vault; blinds had to be drawn up, and glass cases uncovered, before we could see a thing except the row of murderers' death-masks—the placid faces with the swollen necks—that stood out on their shelves to give us ghostly greeting.

"This fellow isn't formidable," whispered Raffles, as the blinds went up; "still, we can't be too careful. My little lot are round the corner, in the sort of recess; don't look till we come to them in their turn."

So we began at the beginning, with the glass case nearest the door; and in a moment I discovered that I knew far more about its contents than our pallid guide. He had some enthusiasm, but the most inaccurate smattering of his subject. He mixed up the first murderer with quite the wrong murder, and capped his mistake in the next breath with an intolerable libel on the very pearl of our particular tribe.

"This revawlver," he began, "belonged to the celebrited burgular, Chawles Peace. These are his spectacles, that's his jimmy, and this here knife's the one that Chawley killed the policeman with."

Now I like accuracy for its own sake, strive after it myself, and am sometimes guilty of forcing it upon others. So this was more than I could pass.

"That's not quite right," I put in mildly. "He never made use of the knife."

The young clerk twisted his head round in its vase of starch.

"Chawley Peace killed two policemen," said he.

"No, he didn't; only one of them was a policeman; and he never killed anybody with a knife."

The clerk took the correction like a lamb. I could not have refrained from making it, to save my skin. But Raffles rewarded me with as vicious a little kick as he could administer unobserved. "Who was Charles Peace?" he inquired, with the bland effrontery of any judge upon the bench.

The clerk's reply came pat and unexpected. "The greatest burgular we ever had," said he, "till good old Raffles knocked him out!"

"The greatest of the pre-Raffleites," the master murmured, as we passed on to the safer memorials of mere murder. There were misshapen bullets and stained knives that had taken human life; there were lithe, lean ropes which had retaliated after the live letter of the Mosaic law. There was one bristling broadside of revolvers under the longest shelf of closed eyes and swollen throats. There were festoons of rope-ladders—none so ingenious as ours—and then at last there was something that the clerk knew all. about. It was a small tin cigarette-box, and the name upon the gaudy wrapper was not the name of Sullivan. Yet Raffles and I knew even more about this exhibit than the clerk.

"There, now," said our guide, "you'll never guess the history of that! I'll give you twenty guesses, and the twentieth will be no nearer than the first"

"I'm sure of it, my good fellow," rejoined Raffles, a discreet twinkle in his eye. "Tell us about it, to save time."

And he opened, as he spoke, his own old twenty-five tin of purely popular cigarettes; there were a few in it still, but between the cigarettes were jammed lumps of sugar wadded with cotton-wool. I saw Raffles weighing the lot in his hand with subtle satisfaction. But the clerk saw merely the mystification which he desired to create.

"I thought that'd beat you, sir," said he. "It was an American dodge. Two smart Yankees got a jeweller to take a lot of stuff to a private room at Keliner's, where they were dining, for them to choose from. When it came to paying, there was some bother about a remittance; but they soon made that all. right, for they were far too clever to suggest taking away what they'd chosen but couldn't pay for. No, all. they wanted was that what they'd chosen might be locked up in the safe and considered theirs until their money came for them to pay for it. All. they asked was to seal the stuff up in something; the jeweller was to take it away and not meddle with it, nor yet break the seals, for a week or two. It seemed a fair enough thing, now, didn't it, sir?"

"Eminently fair," said Raffles sententiously.

"So the jeweller thought," crowed the clerk. "You see, it wasn't as if the Yanks had chosen out the half of what he'd brought on appro.; they'd gone slow on purpose, and they'd paid for all. they could on the nail, just for a blind. Well, I suppose you can guess what happened in the end? The jeweller never heard of those Americans again; and these few cigarettes and lumps of sugar were all. he found."

"Duplicate boxes? I cried, perhaps a thought too promptly.

"Duplicate boxes!" murmured Raffles, as profoundly impressed as a second Mr. Pickwick.

"Duplicate boxes!" echoed the triumphant clerk. "Artful beggars, these Americans, sir! You've got to crawss the 'Erring Pond to learn a trick worth one o' that?"

"I suppose so," assented the grave gentleman wit the silver hair. "Unless," he added, as if suddenly inspired, "unless it was that man Raffles."

"It couldn't 've bin," jerked the clerk from his conning-tower of a collar. "He'd gone to Davy Jones long before."

"Are you sure?" asked Raffles. "Was his body ever found?"

"Found and buried," replied our imaginative friend. "Malter, I think it was; or it may have been Giberaltar. I forget which."

"Besides," I put in, rather annoyed at all. this wilful work, yet not indisposed to make a late contribution—"besides, Raffles would never have smoked those cigarettes. There was only one brand for him. It was—let me see—"

"Sullivans? cried the clerk, right for once. "It's all. a matter of 'abit," he went on, as he replaced the twenty-five tin box with the vulgar wrapper. "I tried them once, and I didn't like 'em myself. It's all. a question of taste. Now, if you want a good smoke, and cheaper, give me a Golden Gem at quarter of the price."

"What we really do want," remarked Raffles mildly, "is to see something else as clever as that last."

"Then come this way," said the clerk, and led us into a recess almost monopolized by the iron-clamped chest of thrilling memory, now a mere platform for the collection of mysterious objects under a dust-sheet on the lid. "These," he continued, unveiling them with an air, are the Raffles Relics, taken from his rooms in the Albany after his death and burial, and the most complete set we've got. That's his centre-bit, and this is the bottle of rock-oil he's supposed to have kept dipping it in to prevent making a noise. Here's the revawlver he used when he shot at a gentleman on the roof down Horsham way; it was afterward taken from him on the P. & 0. boat before he jumped overboard."

I could not help saying I understood that Raffles had never shot at anybody. I was standing with my back to the nearest window, my hat jammed over my brows and my overcoat collar up to my ears.

"That's the only time we know about," the clerk admitted; "and it couldn't be brought 'ome, or his precious pal would have got more than he did. This empty cawtridge is the one he 'id the Emperor's pearl in, on the Peninsular and Orient. These gimlets and wedges were what he used for fixin' doors. This is his rope-ladder, with the telescope walking-stick he used to hook it up with; he's said to have 'ad it with him the night he dined with the Earl of Thornaby, and robbed the house before dinner. That's his life-preserver; but no one can make out what this little thick velvet bag's for, with the two holes and the elawstic round each. Perhaps you can give a guess, sir?"

Raffles had taken up the bag that he had invented for the noiseless filing of keys. Now he handled it as though it were a tobacco-pouch, putting in finger and thumb, and shrugging over the puzzle with a delicious face; nevertheless, he showed me a few grains of steel filing as the result of his investigations, and murmured in my ear, "These sweet police! I, for my part, could not but examine the life-preserver with which I had once smitten Raffles himself to the ground: actually, there was his blood upon it still; and seeing my horror, the clerk plunged into a characteristically garbled version of that incident also. It happened to have come to light among others at the Old Bailey, and perhaps had its share in promoting the quality of mercy which had undoubtedly been exercised on my behalf. But the present recital was unduly trying, and Raffles created a noble diversion by calling attention to an early photograph of himself, which may still hang on the wall over the historic chest, but which I had carefully ignored. It shows him in flannels, after some great feat upon the tented field. I am afraid there is a Sullivan between his lips, a look of lazy insolence in the half-shut eyes. I have since possessed myself of a copy, and it is not Raffles at his best; but the features are clean-cut and regular; and I often wish that I had lent it to the artistic gentlemen who have battered the statue out of all. likeness to the man.

"You wouldn't think it of him, would you?" quoth the clerk. "It makes you understand how no one ever did think it of him at the time."

The youth was looking full at Raffles, with the watery eyes of unsuspecting innocence. I itched to emulate the fine bravado of my friend.

"You said he had a pal," I observed, sinking deeper into the collar of my coat. "Haven't you got a photograph of him?"

The pale clerk gave such a sickly smile, I could have smacked some blood into his pasty face.

"You mean Bunny?" said the familiar fellow. "No, sir, he'd be out of place; we've only room for real criminals here. Bunny was neither one thing nor the other. He could follow Raffles, but that's all. he could do. He was no good on his own. Even when he put up the low-down job of robbing his old 'ome, it's believed he hadn't the 'eart to take the stuff away, and Raffles had to break in a second time for it. No, sir, we don't bother our heads about Bunny; we shall never hear no more of 'im. He was a harmless sort of rotter, if you awsk me."

I had not asked him, and I was almost foaming under the respirator that I was making of my overcoat collar. I only hoped that Raffles would say something, and he did.

"The only case I remember anything about," he remarked, tapping the clamped chest with his umbrella, "was this; and that time, at all. events, the man outside must have had quite as much to do as the one inside. May I ask what you keep in it?"

"Nothing, sir.

"I imagined more relics inside. Hadn't he some dodge of getting in and out without opening the lid?"

"Of putting his head out, you mean," returned the clerk, whose knowledge of Raffles and his Relics was really most comprehensive on the whole. He moved some of the minor memorials and with his penknife raised the trap-door in the lid.

"Only a skylight," remarked Raffles, deliciously unimpressed.

"Why, what else did you expect?" asked the clerk, letting the trap-door down again, and looking sorry that he had taken so much trouble.

"A backdoor, at least!" replied Raffles, with such a sly look at me that I had to turn aside to smile. It was the last time I smiled that day.

The door had opened as I turned, and an unmistakable detective had entered with two more sight-seers like ourselves. He wore the hard, round hat and the dark, thick overcoat which one knows at a glance as the uniform of his grade; and for one awful moment his steely eye was upon us in a flash of cold inquiry. Then the clerk emerged from the recess devoted to the Raffles Relics, and the alarming interloper conducted his party to the window opposite the door.

"Inspector Druce," the clerk informed us in impressive whispers, "who had the Chalk Farm case in hand. He'd be the man for Raffles, if Raffles was alive to-day!"

"I'm sure he would," was the grave reply. "I should be very sorry to have a man like that after me. But what a run there seems to be upon your Black Museum!"

"There isn't reelly, sir," whispered the clerk. "We sometimes go weeks on end without having regular visitors like you two gentlemen. I think those are friends of the Inspector's, come to see the Chalk Farm photographs, that helped to hang his man. We've a lot of interesting photographs, sir, if you like to have a look at them."

"If it won't take long," said Raffles, taking out his watch; and as the clerk left our side for an instant he gripped my arm. "This is a bit too hot," he whispered, "but we mustn't cut and run like rabbits. That might be fatal. Hide your face in the photographs, and leave everything to me. I'll have a train to catch as soon as ever I dare."

I obeyed without a word, and with the less uneasiness as I had time to consider the situation. It even struck me that Raffles was for once inclined to exaggerate the undeniable risk that we ran by remaining in the same room with an officer whom both he and I knew only too well by name and repute. Raffles, after all., had aged and altered out of knowledge; but he had not lost the nerve that was equal to a far more direct encounter than was at all. likely to be forced upon us. On the other hand, it was most improbable that a distinguished detective would know by sight an obscure delinquent like myself; besides, this one had come to the front since my day. Yet a risk it was, and I certainly did not smile as I bent over the album of horrors produced by our guide. I could still take an interest in the dreadful photographs of murderous and murdered men; they appealed to the morbid element in my nature; and it was doubtless with degenerate unction that I called Raffles's attention to a certain scene of notorious slaughter. There was no response. I looked round. There was no Raffles to respond. We had all. three been examining the photographs at one of the windows; at another three newcomers were similarly engrossed; and without one word, or a single sound, Raffles had decamped behind all. our backs.

Fortunately the clerk was himself very busy gloating over the horrors of the album; before he looked round I had hidden my astonishment, but not my wrath, of which I had the instinctive sense to make no secret.

"My friend's the most impatient man on earth!" I exclaimed. "He said he was going to catch a train, and now he's gone without a word!"

"I never heard him," said the clerk, looking puzzled.

"No more did I; but he did touch me on the shoulder," I lied, "and say something or other. I was too deep in this beastly book to pay much attention. He must have meant that he was off. Well, let him be off! I mean to see all. that's to be seen."

And in my nervous anxiety to allay any suspicions aroused by my companion's extraordinary behavior, I outstayed even the eminent detective and his friends, saw them examine the Raffles Relics, heard them discuss me under my own nose, and at last was alone with the anemic clerk. I put my hand in my pocket, and measured him with a sidelong eye. The tipping system is nothing less than a minor bane of my existence. Not that one is a grudging giver, but simply because in so many cases it is so hard to know whom to tip and what to tip him. I know what it is to be the parting guest who has not parted freely enough, and that not from stinginess but the want of a fine instinct on the point. I made no mistake, however, in the case of the clerk, who accepted my pieces of silver without demur, and expressed a hope of seeing the article which I had assured him I was about to write. He has had some years to wait for it, but I flatter myself that these belated pages will occasion more interest than offense if they ever do meet those watery eyes.

Twilight was falling when I reached the street; the sky behind St. Stephen's had flushed and blackened like an angry face; the lamps were lit, and under every one I was unreasonable enough to look for Raffles. Then I made foolishly sure that I should find him hanging about the station, and hung thereabouts myself until one Richmond train had gone without me. In the end I walked over the bridge to Waterloo, and took the first train to Teddington instead. That made a shorter walk of it, but I had to grope my way through a white fog from the river to Ham Common, and it was the hour of our cosy dinner when I reached our place of retirement. There was only a flicker of firelight on the blinds: I was the first to return after all. It was nearly four hours since Raffles had stolen away from my side in the ominous precincts of Scotland Yard. Where could he be? Our landlady wrung her hands over him; she had cooked a dinner after her favorite's heart, and I let it spoil before making one of the most melancholy meals of my life.

Up to midnight there was no sign of him; but long before this time I had reassured our landlady with a voice and face that must have given my words the lie. I told her that Mr. Ralph (as she used to call him) had said something about going to the theatre; that I thought he had given up the idea, but I must have been mistaken, and should certainly sit up for him. The attentive soul brought in a plate of sandwiches before she retired; and I prepared to make a night of it in a chair by the sitting-room fire. Darkness and bed I could not face in my anxiety. In a way I felt as though duty and loyalty called me out into the winter s night; and yet whither should I turn to look for Raffles? I could think of but one place, and to seek him there would be to destroy myself without aiding him. It was my growing conviction that he had been recognized when leaving Scotland Yard, and either taken then and there, or else hunted into some new place of hiding. It would all. be in the morning papers; and it was all. his own fault. He had thrust his head into the lion's mouth, and the lion's jaws had snapped. Had he managed to withdraw his head in time?

There was a bottle at my elbow, and that night I say deliberately that it was not my enemy but my friend. It procured me at last some surcease from my suspense. I fell fast asleep in my chair before the fire. The lamp was still burning, and the fire red, when I awoke; but I sat very stiff in the iron clutch of a wintry morning. Suddenly I slued round in my chair. And there was Raffles in a chair behind me, with the door open behind him, quietly taking off his boots.

"Sorry to wake you, Bunny," said he. "I thought I was behaving like a mouse; but after a three hours' tramp one's feet are all. heels."

I did not get up and fall upon his neck. I sat back in my chair and blinked with bitterness upon his selfish insensibility. He should not know what I had been through on his account.

"Walk out from town?" I inquired, as indifferently as though he were in the habit of doing so.

"From Scotland Yard," he answered, stretching himself before the fire in his stocking soles.

"Scotland Yard?" I echoed. "Then I was right; that's where you were all. the time; and yet you managed to escape!"

I had risen excitedly in my turn.

"Of course I did," replied Raffles. "I never thought there would be much difficulty about that, but there was even less than I anticipated. I did once find myself on one side of a sort of counter, and an officer dozing at his desk at the other side. I thought it safest to wake him up and make inquiries about a mythical purse left in a phantom hansom outside the Carlton. And the way the fellow fired me out of that was another credit to the Metropolitan Police: it's only in the savage countries that they would have troubled to ask how one had got in."

"And how did you?" I asked. "And in the Lord's name, Raffles, when and why?"

Raffles looked down on me under raised eyebrows, as he stood with his coat tails to the dying fire.

"How and when, Bunny, you know as well as I do," said he, cryptically. "And at last you shall hear the honest why and wherefore. I had more reasons for going to Scotland Yard, my dear fellow, than I had the face to tell you at the time."

"I don't care why you went there!" I cried. "I want to know why you stayed, or went back, or whatever it was you may have done. I thought they had got you, and you had given them the slip!"

Raffles smiled as he shook his head.

"No, no, Bunny; I prolonged the visit, as I paid it, of my own accord. As for my reasons, they are far too many for me to tell you them all.; they rather weighed upon me as I walked out; but you'll see them for yourself if you turn round."

I was standing with my back to the chair in which I had been asleep; behind the chair was the round lodging-house table; and there, reposing on the cloth with the whiskey and sandwiches, was the whole collection of Raffles Relics which had occupied the lid of the silver-chest in the Black Museum at Scotland Yard! The chest alone was missing. There was the revolver that I had only once heard fired, and there the blood-stained life-preserver, brace-and-bit, bottle of rock-oil, velvet bag, rope-ladder, walking-stick, gimlets, wedges, and even the empty cartridge-case which had once concealed the gift of a civilized monarch to a potentate of color.

"I was a real Father Christmas," said Raffles, "when I arrived. It's a pity you weren't awake to appreciate the scene. It was more edifying than the one I found. You never caught me asleep in my chair, Bunny!"

He thought I had merely fallen asleep in my chair! He could not see that I had been sitting up for him all. night long! The hint of a temperance homily, on top of all. I had borne, and from Raffles of all. mortal men, tried my temper to its last limit—but a flash of late enlightenment enabled me just to keep it.

"Where did you hide?" I asked grimly.

"At the Yard itself."

"So I gather; but whereabouts at the Yard?"

"Can you ask, Bunny?"

"I am asking."

"It's where I once hid before."

"You don't mean in the chest?"

"I do."

Our eyes met for a minute.

"You may have ended up there," I conceded. "But where did you go first when you slipped out behind my back, and how the devil did you know where to go?"

"I never did slip out," said Raffles, "behind your back. I slipped in."

"Into the chest?"

"Exactly."

I burst out laughing in his face.

"My dear fellow, I saw all. these things on the lid just afterward. Not one of them was moved. I watched that detective show them to his friends."

"And I heard him."

"But not from the inside of the chest?"

"From the inside of the chest, Bunny. Don't look like that—it's foolish. Try to recall a few words that went before, between the idiot in the collar and me. Don't you remember my asking him if there was anything in the chest?"

"Yes."

"One had to be sure it was empty, you see. Then I asked if there was a backdoor to the chest as well as a skylight."

"I remember."

"I suppose you thought all. that meant nothing?"

"I didn't look for a meaning."

"You wouldn't; it would never occur to you that I might want to find out whether anybody at the Yard had found out that there was something precisely in the nature of a sidedoor—it isn't a backdoor—to that chest. Well, there is one; there was one soon after I took the chest back from your rooms to mine, in the good old days. You push one of the handles down—which no one ever does—and the whole of that end opens like the front of a doll's house. I saw that was what I ought to have done at first: it's so much simpler than the trap at the top; and one likes to get a thing perfect for its own sake. Besides, the trick had not been spotted at the bank, and I thought I might bring it off again some day; meanwhile, in one's bedroom, with lots of things on top, what a port in a sudden squall!"

I asked why I had never heard of the improvement before, not so much at the time it was made, but in these later days, when there were fewer secrets between us, and this one could avail him no more. But I did not put the question out of pique. I put it out of sheer obstinate incredulity. And Raffles looked at me without replying, until I read the explanation in his look.

"I see," I said. "You used to get into it to hide from me!"

"My dear Bunny, I am not always a very genial man," he answered; "but when you let me have a key of your rooms I could not very well refuse you one of mine, although I picked your pocket of it in the end. I will only say that when I had no wish to see you, Bunny, I must have been quite unfit for human society, and it was the act of a friend to deny you mine. I don't think it happened more than once or twice. You can afford to forgive a fellow after all. these years?

"That, yes," I replied bitterly; "but not this, Raffles."

"Why not? I really hadn't made up my mind to do what I did. I had merely thought of it. It was that smart officer in the same room that made me do it without thinking twice."

"And we never even heard you!" I murmured, in a voice of involuntary admiration which vexed me with myself. "But we might just as well!" I was as quick to add in my former tone.

"Why, Bunny?"

"We shall be traced in no time through our ticket of admission."

"Did they collect it?"

"No; but you heard how very few are issued."

"Exactly. They sometimes go weeks on end without a regular visitor. It was I who extracted that piece of information, Bunny, and I did nothing rash until I had. Don't you see that with any luck it will be two or three weeks before they are likely to discover their loss?"

I was beginning to see.

"And then, pray, how are they going to bring it home to us? Why should they even suspect us, Bunny? I left early; that's all. I did. You took my departure admirably; you couldn't have said more or less if I had coached you myself. I relied on you, Bunny, and you never more completely justified my confidence. The sad thing is that you have ceased to rely on me. Do you really think that I would leave the place in such a state that the first person who came in with a duster would see that there had been a robbery?"

I denied the thought with all. energy, though it perished only as I spoke.

"Have you forgotten the duster that was over these things, Bunny? Have you forgotten all. the other revolvers and life preservers that there were to choose from? I chose most carefully, and I replaced my relics with a mixed assortment of other people's which really look just as well. The rope-ladder that now supplants mine is, of course, no patch upon it, but coiled up on the chest it really looks much the same. To be sure, there was no second velvet bag; but I replaced my stick with another quite like it, and I even found an empty cartridge to understudy the setting of the Polynesian pearl. You see the sort of fellow they have to show people round: do you think he's the kind to see the difference next time, or to connect it with us if he does? One left much the same things, lying much as he left them, under a dust-sheet which is only taken off for the benefit of the curious, who often don't turn up for weeks on end."

I admitted that we might be safe for three or four weeks. Raffles held out his hand.

"Then let us be friends about it, Bunny, and smoke the cigarette of Sullivan and peace! A lot may happen in three or four weeks; and what should you say if this turned out to be the last as well as the least of all. my crimes? I must own that it seems to me their natural and fitting end, though I might have stopped more characteristically than with a mere crime of sentiment. No, I make no promises, Bunny; now I have got these things, I may be unable to resist using them once more. But with this war one gets all. the excitement one requires— and rather more than usual may happen in three or four weeks?"

Was he thinking even then of volunteering for the front? Had he already set his heart on the one chance of some atonement for his life—nay, on the very death he was to die? I never knew, and shall never know. Yet his words were strangely prophetic, even to the three or four weeks in which those events happened that imperilled the fabric of our empire, and rallied her sons from the four winds to fight beneath her banner on the veldt. It all. seems very ancient history now. But I remember nothing better or more vividly than the last words of Raffles upon his last crime, unless it be the pressure of his hand as he said them, or the rather sad twinkle in his tired eyes.

The Last Word

The last of all. these tales of Raffles is from a fresher and a sweeter pen. I give it exactly as it came to me, in a letter which meant more to me than it can possibly mean to any other reader. And yet, it may stand for something with those for whom these pale reflections have a tithe of the charm that the real man had for me; and it is to leave such persons thinking yet a little better of him (and not wasting another thought on me) that I am permitted to retail the very last word about their hero and mine.

The letter was my first healing after a chance encounter and a sleepless night; and I print every word of it except the last

"39 CAMPDEN GROVE COURT, W.,
"June 28, 1900.

"DEAR HARRY: You may have wondered at the very few words I could find to say to you when we met so strangely yesterday. I did not mean to be unkind. I was grieved to see you so cruelly hurt and lame. I could not grieve when at last I made you tell me how it happened. I honor and envy every man of you—every name in those dreadful lists that fill the papers every day. But I knew about Mr. Raffles, and I did not know about you, and there was something I longed to tell you about him, something I could not tell you in a minute in the street, or indeed by word of mouth at all. That is why I asked you for your address.

"You said I spoke as if I had known Mr. Raffles. Of course I have often seen him playing cricket, and heard about him and you. But I only once met him, and that was the night after you and I met last. I have always supposed that you knew all. about our meeting. Yesterday I could see that you knew nothing. So I have made up my mind to tell you every word.

"That night—I mean the next night—they were all. going out to several places, but I stayed behind at Palace Gardens. I had gone up to the drawing-room after dinner, and was just putting on the lights, when in walked Mr. Raffles from the balcony. I knew him at once, because I happened to have watched him make his hundred at Lord's only the day before. He seemed surprised that no one had told me he was there, but the whole thing was such a surprise that I hardly thought of that. I am afraid I must say that it was not a very pleasant surprise. I felt instinctively that he had come from you, and I confess that for the moment it made me very angry indeed. Then in a breath he assured me that you knew nothing of his coming, that you would never have allowed him to come, but that he had taken it upon himself as your intimate friend and one who would be mine as well. (I said that I would tell you every word.)

"Well, we stood looking at each other for some time, and I was never more convinced of anybody's straightness and sincerity; but he was straight and sincere with me, and true to you that night, whatever he may have been before and after. So I asked him why he had come, and what had happened; and he said it was not what had happened, but what might happen next; so I asked him if he was thinking of you, and he just nodded, and told me that I knew very well what you had done. But I began to wonder whether Mr. Raffles himself knew, and I tried to get him to tell me what you had done, and he said I knew as well as he did that you were one of the two men who had come to the house the night before. I took some time to answer. I was quite mystified by his manner. At last I asked him how he knew. I can hear his answer now.

"'Because I was the other man,' he said quite quietly; 'because I led him blindfold into the whole business, and would rather pay the shot than see poor Bunny suffer for it.'

"Those were his words, but as he said them he made their meaning clear by going over to the bell, and waiting with his finger ready to ring for whatever assistance or protection I desired. Of course I would not let him ring at all.; in fact, at first I refused to believe him. Then he led me out into the balcony, and showed me exactly how he had got up and in. He had broken in for the second night running, and all. to tell me that the first night he had brought you with him on false pretences. He had to tell me a great deal more before I could quite believe him. But before he went (as he had come) I was the one woman in the world who knew that A. J. Raffles, the great cricketer, and the so-called 'amateur cracksman' of equal notoriety, were one and the same person.

"He had told me his secret, thrown himself on my mercy, and put his liberty if not his life in my hands, but all. for your sake, Harry, to right you in my eyes at his own expense. And yesterday I could see that you knew nothing whatever about it, that your friend had died without telling you of his act of real and yet vain self-sacrifice! Harry, I can only say that now I understand your friendship, and the dreadful lengths to which it carried you. How many in your place would not have gone as far for such a friend? Since that night, at any rate, I for one have understood. It has grieved me more than I can tell you, Harry, but I have always understood.

"He spoke to me quite simply and frankly of his life. It was wonderful to me then that he should speak of it as he did, and still more wonderful that I should sit and listen to him as I did. But I have often thought about it since, and have long ceased to wonder at myself. There was an absolute magnetism about Mr. Raffles which neither you nor I could resist. He had the strength of personality which is a different thing from strength of character; but when you meet both kinds together, they carry the ordinary mortal off his or her feet. You must not imagine you are the only one who would have served and followed him as you did. When he told me it was all. a game to him, and the one game he knew that was always exciting, always full of danger and of drama, I could just then have found it in my heart to try the game myself! Not that he treated me to any ingenious sophistries or paradoxical perversities. It was just his natural charm and humor, and a touch of sadness with it all., that appealed to something deeper than one's reason and one's sense of right. Glamour, I suppose, is the word. Yet there was far more in him than that. There were depths, which called to depths; and you will not misunderstand me when I say I think it touched him that a woman should listen to him as I did, and in such circumstances. I know that it touched me to think of such a life so spent, and that I came to myself and implored him to give it all. up. I don't think I went on my knees over it. But I am afraid I did cry; and that was the end. He pretended not to notice anything, and then in an instant he froze everything with a flippancy which jarred horribly at the time, but has ever since touched me more than all. the rest. I remember that I wanted to shake hands at the end. But Mr. Raffles only shook his head, and for one instant his face was as sad as it was gallant and gay all. the rest of the time. Then he went as he had come, in his own dreadful way, and not a soul in the house knew that he had been. And even you were never told!

"I didn't mean to write all. this about your own friend, whom you knew so much better yourself, yet you see that even you did not know how nobly he tried to undo the wrong he had done you; and now I think I know why he kept it to himself. It is fearfully late—or early—I seem to have been writing all. night— and I will explain the matter in the fewest words. I promised Mr. Raffles that I would write to you, Harry, and see you if I could. Well, I did write, and I did mean to see you, but I never had an answer to what I wrote. It was only one line, and I have long known you never received it. I could not bring myself to write more, and even those few words were merely slipped into one of the books which you had given me. Years afterward these books, with my name in them, must have been found in your rooms; at any rate they were returned to me by somebody; and you could never have opened them, for there was my line where I had left it. Of course you had never seen it, and that was all. my fault. But it was too late to write again. Mr. Raffles was supposed to have been drowned, and everything was known about you both. But I still kept my own independent knowledge to myself; to this day, no one else knows that you were one of the two in Palace Gardens; and I still blame myself more than you may think for nearly everything that has happened since.

"You said yesterday that your going to the war and getting wounded wiped out nothing that had gone before. I hope you are not growing morbid about the past. It is not for me to condone it, and yet I know that Mr. Raffles was what he was because he loved danger and adventure, and that you were what you were because you loved Mr. Raffles. But, even admitting it was all. as bad as bad could be, he is dead, and you are punished. The world forgives, if it does not forget. You are young enough to live everything down. Your part in the war will help you in more ways than one. You were always fond of writing. You have now enough to write about for a literary lifetime. You must make a new name for yourself. You must Harry, and you will!

"I suppose you know that my aunt, Lady Melrose, died some years ago? She was the best friend I had in the world, and it is thanks to her that I am living my own life now in the one way after my own heart. This is a new block of flats, one of those where they do everything for you; and though mine is tiny, it is more than all. I shall ever want. One does just exactly what one likes—and you must blame that habit for all. that is least conventional in what I have said. Yet I should like you to understand why it is that I have said so much, and, indeed, left nothing unsaid. It is because I want never to have to say or hear another word about anything that is past and over. You may answer that I run no risk! Nevertheless, if you did care to come and see me some day as an old friend, we might find one or two new points of contact, for I am rather trying to write myself! You might almost guess as much from this letter; it is long enough for anything; but, Harry, if it makes you realize that one of your oldest friends is glad to have seen you, and will be gladder still to see you again, and to talk of anything and everything except the past, I shall cease to be ashamed even of its length!

"And so good-by for the present from

"——"

I omit her name and nothing else. Did I not say in the beginning that it should never be sullied by association with mine? And yet—and yet—even as I write I have a hope in my heart of hearts which is not quite consistent with that sentiment. It is as faint a hope as man ever had, and yet its audacity makes the pen tremble in my fingers. But, if it be ever realized, I shall owe more than I could deserve in a century of atonement to one who atoned more nobly than I ever can. And to think that to the end I never heard one word of it from Raffles!

Lightning Source UK Ltd.
Milton Keynes UK
UKHW03f0949190318
319635UK00001BA/47/P